MORMON EROTICA

MORMON EROTICA

DONNA BANTA

MORMON ALUMNI
ASSOCIATION
Gone for Good

MORMON ALUMNI
ASSOCIATION
Gone for Good

MORMON ALUMNI ASSOCIATION LLC
mormonalumniassociation.org

MORMON EROTICA
Copyright © 2018 by Donna Banta. All rights reserved.

ISBN
978-0-9900170-2-8

Cover art by
C.L. Hanson

Contact the author at donna.banta@gmail.com

Acknowledgements

I would like to thank Johnny Townsend, Mark Piper, Ruth Wildes Schuler, Jon Shearer, Jennifer Gowans-Vandenberg, and C.L. Hanson for their invaluable help.

For my husband, Mark,
who refuses to mix and mingle

1

I should have seen it coming. The warning signs were all there. After forty-five years of adhering to my faith, I fell dismally short of the Mormon ideal. I was a scientist in a world of magical thinking, a divorced single dad in a culture that prized marriage and family, a chronic grumbler in a roomful of mixing and mingling. In hindsight, I was a disaster waiting to happen. But at the time, I hadn't a clue. The problem was I'd been complacent, too settled in my situation, blind to the danger simmering around me. Sort of like the frog in that old Sunday School analogy, the one who didn't know the pot was about to boil. That was me. Languishing in my own stew.

So, as unbelievable as it now seems, only three weeks ago today I was sticking with the same old drill, content with my single, celibate existence, wholly unaware that my life was about to be turned upside down, and that nothing less than my eternal happiness was to be at stake.

2

Bishop Franklin's home looked like every other in San Jose's Almaden Valley, a white stucco California ranch style with the obligatory bougainvillea climbing up the chimney. I rolled down the driver's side window of my Toyota Prius to let in the warm, early October breeze. Minutes later, the front door swung open and a river of teenaged Mormon girls flooded the threshold and front walk.

Julia climbed in the passenger side and buckled her seatbelt. I smiled over at the kid, anxious to claim what was left of our regular Wednesday evening. "How was the Bishop's Standards Night?"

She frowned. "Fine, Dad."

Her friend Marnie passed by my window. "Hi, Brother Maxwell," she said, even though I'd invited her to call me Jim.

"Hello, Sister Frost," I replied, and then to Julia. "Only fine, kiddo?"

"Yeah," she mumbled, her eyes aimed downward.

We pulled away from the curb and rode in silence across San Jose, from the Almaden Valley where Julia lived and attended church with her mother, to Willow Glen where she stayed with me. I parked in my driveway and she broke into tears. Unhooking my seatbelt, I rested my hand against the back of her neck. Her skin was moist from perspiration and her ponytail brushed against my knuckles.

"Honey, what's wrong?"

"I don't want to do my interview with Bishop Franklin this month."

"Why not?"

"I don't like him."

"He's new. You're not used to him yet." I handed her my handkerchief.

She dabbed her eyes and made that face she wore when I used to untangle her hair with a comb. I knew better than to force a conversation with my fourteen-year-old.

"Okay," I said. "There are people I don't like, too."

"Mom says that's why you work from home."

I rolled my eyes. "Let's go inside."

As we walked into the kitchen, I thought of my one-on-ones with Bishop Haas in my Willow Glen ward, awkward exchanges over my absence from the single adult activities.

"Come here." I kissed Julia's forehead and hugged her. She was already five-foot-eight, barely an inch shorter than me, and model-thin like her mother. "Maybe you'll end up working at home."

Her eyes darted up at mine. "So you won't make me meet with him?"

"Of course I won't *make* you."

"Thanks, Dad."

"Do you have homework?"

"Done."

"Popcorn and *Harry Potter*, then?"

She answered with the crooked grin she'd inherited from me.

After the movie, Julia went to bed and I paced the kitchen, worrying. It didn't feel right to make my daughter talk to her bishop. Only her anxiety over the suggestion signaled a red flag. Could it be she *needed* to talk to him? Was a boy in her ward pressuring her to go too far? Julia wasn't allowed to date until she turned sixteen, and if she'd shown the slightest hint of interaction with a kid in the Almaden ward my ex, Whitney, would be on to them. A nonmember boy at school seemed more likely. But when and where would they sneak off? Whitney and I kept tabs on her after school. If she skipped class, the principal would call.

Then it hit me. Maybe it wasn't a boy.

It wasn't a far-fetched notion. Sometimes I wondered if Whitney preferred women. Other times I figured she hated sex altogether. But generally I concluded that she hated me. I thought again of my talks with Bishop Haas. What he couldn't grasp was that I no longer had faith in the institution of marriage. My testimony of the restored gospel remained firm. But when it came to weddings, I was agnostic.

3

It was past two a.m. on Thursday morning before I fell asleep. We were up again at five, fumbling through our morning chores and rushing back to Almaden Valley for Julia's early morning seminary class.

"Awake yet, kiddo?" I asked as we cruised down the expressway.

"Barely."

"First Corinthians, chapter six, verses twenty through twenty-two."

Julia yawned. "Dad, we're not even close to reading First Corinthians yet."

"So? It's a Scripture Mastery scripture. Here's the hint. *Your body is a temple.*"

I looked over to see if that particular topic inspired any guilty discomfort. Her eyes were closed and her head rested against the passenger side window. No trace of a reaction.

"Can't I just read the New Testament without memorizing?" she asked finally.

"Memorization cements things in your mind, kiddo. So you can rock at the scripture chase games."

"I'm not really into games, Dad. Brother Price says that's okay, so long as we keep up with the assigned reading."

Feeling somewhat rejected, I turned off the expressway. "Guess I shouldn't have bothered designing that little app for your phone."

Julia roused herself and hoisted her backpack into her lap. "I like the app, Dad." She sent a sleepy smile in my direction. "And I love that you made it for me."

"If you hit 'shuffle scriptures' the verses pop up out of order, keep you on your toes."

"I know." She yawned again. "It's very clever. Much better than the app the Church offers. You should sell it. Make some money."

Sighing, I pulled into the church lot and parked. "Marnie's mom is giving you a ride to school after, right?"

Julia moaned, "Yes, Dad," and was out the door before I could say, "Bye, kiddo." Watching her dash inside the building, I was reminded of how I had to sneak away from her preschool before she saw and burst into tears. What a difference a decade made.

I was backing out of my parking space when the phone rang. Kellie. I hit "accept" on my dash.

"Sis."

"Where are you?"

"Almaden Valley."

"In that eco-fascist car of yours?"

I made a right onto Almaden Expressway. "Owning a Prius does not make me an eco-fascist."

"I dreamt about Mom last night," she said.

"Oh, yeah? Me, too. Must be a slow week in the Spirit World."

"She told me you're about to find *the one*."

"She says that in all of my dreams."

"Not in mine. In my dreams she tells me to lighten up on Craig and the boys."

"Well, she's right about Craig and my nephews, but wrong about me."

"She also said you'll meet this girl in an unlikely place."

"Said that to me, too." I paused to process this. "Like where? That salsa dance class she tried to get me into before she died?"

"Maybe you should finally take her up on it."

"I don't do much that's unlikely anymore, Kel."

"Coming for dinner Sunday?"

I pulled to a stop and punched the park button. "Yup, and now I'm going to work."

"You're home already?"

"Starbucks."

"I thought you decided to quit going there."

"No. You decided I'd quit going there, even though you know

I never drink their coffee."

"But people see you drinking out of their cups. Go home instead. Or to an office where you're not distracted by all that twittering."

"You mean tweeting."

"At Women's Conference we learned that Satan uses social media to lure us away from Heavenly Father."

"I promise not to follow Satan's tweets when I'm at Starbucks."

"You should stay out of Starbucks."

"What if Miss Right is inside? That could be an unlikely place."

She hesitated, as if considering. "You can't find a decent woman at Starbucks."

"Wrong again. Marcia Costello is meeting me here this morning."

"Marcia—is she still a lesbian?"

I loved my sister, but sometimes she forced me to hold onto my sanity with both hands. "Marcia and her partner of fifteen years recently married."

"I saw pictures of people like them at City Hall. After all our hard work. The court did that to persecute us."

"No."

"It was the anti-Mormon decision."

"They aren't anti-Mormons, they just disagreed—" I massaged my temples. "We obviously differ on this, so—"

"Yes, we do. I stand for righteousness in holy places and you, well, how can I put it?"

"I sit around Starbucks drinking hot chocolate with lesbians?"

"Exactly."

"See you on Sunday, Kel."

"Goodbye, Jimmy."

As I waited in line at the counter, I thought back to when we were kids. Kellie had looked up to me. I was older and, in her mind, wiser. The lone offspring of a single mother, we were something of an anomaly growing up alongside traditional Mormon families, each with two perfect parents and a gaggle of kids. For some reason—perhaps my lack of social skills—this posed less of an embarrassment to me than it did to her. Likewise the chunky thighs we'd inherited from our absent father. Both of us had been late to marry, by Mormon standards anyway, another anomaly that I weathered better than she did. But after my divorce our roles shifted. With my status reduced to single parent, she managed to become the older sibling. Then when Mom died she jumped from older sibling to parent. It never occurred to me to challenge this realignment. Ever since my marriage failed, I'd had trouble weathering the anomalies.

I bought a *New York Times* and found my usual table. Pulling my phone from my shirt pocket, I switched it to pulse mode and then hit shuffle on the app I'd made for Julia. John, chapter fourteen, verse fifteen. "If ye love me, keep my commandments." The shortest of the twenty-five scriptures on the mastery list. At the very least I could get the kid to learn that one. I pocketed the phone and opened the *Times*.

It took me almost an hour to complete the Thursday crossword in pencil. Just as I finished, Marcia swished through the door. She kissed me on my bald spot, pulled the crossword out of her bag, and tossed it on the table beside mine. As always, she had completed her puzzle in pen. Beneath it she'd written, *35 minutes*.

"My treat. What would you like?" she asked. There was a new streak of purple in her short platinum hair.

"Mint tea."

When Marcia returned I noticed something brighter about her appearance, more than just the hair. "You look happy."

Her smile widened. "Cathy and I are going to adopt."

"Fantastic, when?"

She stirred sugar into her coffee. "We just applied. I don't want to jinx it by saying more. How's your morning?"

"Another classic exchange with Kellie."

"Did she rant about married lesbians?"

"Also the Supreme Court, eco-fascists, and twittering. You're in good company."

Marcia chuckled. "She stuck by you during your divorce."

"And she feeds me."

"True." Marcia paused to study me. "You seem preoccupied, Jim."

"I'm worried about Julia. Say, when did you first realize you were a lesbian?"

"For crying out loud, I haven't even had my second cup of coffee yet."

"You know me, I get to the point."

"I remember what it was like working with you."

"Thank you for still loving me."

"I wish you'd find another friend to love you, one you could have sleepovers with."

I smiled.

"Do you think your daughter is a lesbian?" she asked.

I recounted last night's conversation.

Marcia shrugged. "Maybe there's a boy, maybe there's a girl, or maybe she just dislikes the new bishop. You won't know until you ask."

"That's what bishops are for, to ask about all those things a kid doesn't want to talk to her parents about."

"But she doesn't want to talk to the bishop, she wants to talk to you."

"I don't want to alienate her."

"Jim, your manners may be rough but your heart's as big as the Pacific Ocean. Talk to her again."

I frowned and picked up my tea. It was still too hot to drink.

The Unabridged Journal of Julia Camilla Maxwell
Thursday, October 10
8:30 p.m.

I need a place to scream and the journal Mom gave me, the one with "Happy Thoughts" written in curlicues on the cover, just doesn't cut it. Especially when she probably reads it. Dad too maybe. I didn't used to think he would but after last night and this morning, who knows? So from now on, my true thoughts are going here, in this secret password protected file on my laptop.

I thought he was cool! Maybe in his mind he is. After all, Dad did say he wouldn't make me talk to Bishop Franklin. Only I picked up on the clues, the tone in his voice, the sideways looks during Harry Potter. What he really meant was, "Why would I have to make you?" Then this morning with the ridiculous scripture app. Your body is a temple. Real subtle, Dad.

The only way he might get me out of meeting with Bishop Franklin is if I give him a good reason. Which obviously can't be the real reason. (4th period.) If I told him the truth he'd die of shock and I'd die of embarrassment. Then when we came back to life he'd **insist** I talk to Bishop Franklin.

And I can forget about going to my totally mental mother. So who then? Ms. Villanova? She was nice and everything, but she hasn't a clue about our standards. Tell my nonmember school counselor I feel guilty for committing a sin and she rolls her eyes, gives me a pamphlet and some free condoms.

No way around it. I've got to come up with an excuse to get out of talking to Franklin. Soon. And it had better be good.

4

For the rest of the week, work consumed my days while Mom monopolized my sleep. Thursday night she was pulling me in my Radio Flyer wagon and saying, "Marcia's right about your heart, Jimmy, and about a sleepover friend." On Friday night, we were on the sofa in the old house on Lambert. I was in my penguin pajamas with the feet. "Tomorrow, Jimmy, you'll know her in a heartbeat."

Then Saturday dawned and I found myself dawdling during my morning shower, hoping the steam might bring some clarity. Had these dreams about Mom been actual visits from the other side? In the past my spiritual experiences hadn't been all that reliable. The prompting that led to my proposal to Whitney, for example.

Still confused, I dressed, went to the kitchen, and was about to open the fridge when I noticed the invitation lodged under a smiley face magnet. Bishop Haas's oldest daughter rode her fiancé piggyback. I checked the date. Tonight. My mother thought I'd find love at a wedding reception? That wasn't just unlikely, it was ludicrous.

I pushed the reception to the back of my mind and immersed myself in work until the sinking sun in my window signaled it was time to dress for the dreaded event. Shutting my laptop, I stared out at the pink and orange sky, wondering, lamely, if I might find an excuse for skipping my bishop's daughter's reception. I pulled out my phone and hit shuffle on the scripture app.

Matthew, chapter five, verse sixteen. "Let your light so shine before men, that they may see your good works, and glorify your Father which is in heaven." Rolling my eyes, I went to the bedroom to prepare myself to go forth and shine.

Seven years ago, in order to lessen the stress surrounding the rare nuptials I forced myself to attend, I went to Target to buy wedding gifts in bulk. Because Whitney used to complain that my fat stomach grossed her out, I decided on bathroom scales. I bought a dozen, wrapped them in silver paper, slapped my name sticker on each, and stored them in the closet. That night I took one down off the shelf. Eight remained. I put on a tie and glumly drove to the church.

It was the same disturbing scene. Crepe paper dangling from the walls, ceiling, and basketball hoops. A wedding cake cut in postage stamp portions beside a vat of fizzy pink punch. People laughing and celebrating. Elevator tunes about mush. I delivered the scale to the gift table and aimed for the line to congratulate the newlyweds. The sooner I got through it, the sooner I'd get out of here.

"Jimmy!"

I sighed. "Sis."

"See how different this is from Marcia and her girlfriend?"

I looked over at the happy couple. Two virgins, barely out of their teens, and completely clueless about what to do with each other tonight. "You have a point."

My sister took my arm. Even in heels she was a full head shorter than me. "I've nothing against lesbians, but they deserve a civil union, not a real marriage."

"There was nothing civil about my marriage."

"I heard their sealing this morning in the Oakland temple was simply beautiful."

My eyes wandered back to the clueless couple. The bride was patting a bridesmaid's pregnant belly while the groom stared slack-jawed and expressionless as the Elders Quorum president pumped his hand. "Sealed for time and all eternity," I repeated, to nobody in particular.

Kellie poked my shoulder. "Speaking of which, I think your Miss Right is here."

"I think you're delusional."

"Remember Lorraine Grace from Third Ward?"

"Sure. She got married and moved to Atlanta."

"She's not married anymore, and she's back in Third Ward."

"I liked her," I admitted.

"She's over by the punch bowl."

I scanned the refreshments until I found Lorraine. "She looks good."

"Reintroduce yourself."

The opening strains of "We've Only Just Begun" assaulted my ears. "I'm going through the line."

Unhooking Kellie's arm from mine, I walked briskly toward the newlyweds before my sister or my mother's ghost could stop me. I was here for one reason, to congratulate my bishop on his daughter's marriage.

"Jim Maxwell?"

I paused. A shiver ran down my spine. I was pretty sure I knew that voice. I turned to see from where. The same chestnut hair, hazel eyes, and creamy complexion; also an extra fifteen or so pounds that filled out the curves of her silky beige dress. Sadie Gordon. My heart hammered inside my chest. Was this my mother's idea of a joke?

"It's me, Sadie. We dated at BYU, remember?"

"Do I *remember*?"

She giggled and those adorable dimples appeared on her cheeks. My mind warned me to escape before Kellie or Bishop Haas saw us together. The rest of me wondered if she could still kiss like she did in college.

"It's been a long—"

"You look great," I exclaimed, cutting her off.

"Thank you," she replied. "Also thanks for accepting my friend request on Facebook."

I nodded and then, collecting myself, asked, "What brings you here?"

"The groom's mom is an old friend, one of the few who didn't disown me after I wrote *that book*."

I rested a hand on the back of my neck. "I hear it's being made into a movie."

"Can you believe it?" she said. "Who knew there'd be an audience for Mormon erotica?"

"Indeed." Out the corner of my eye I saw Kellie looking our way. I grimaced.

Her smile faded. "I should go."

"Please, not yet." I cleared my throat. "Where do you live these days?"

"San Francisco, and you?"

"San Jose. Here in Willow Glen."

Her smile returned. "I heard you finally got married, to everyone's relief."

"Then I got a divorce, to *my* relief."

She laughed, drawing the attention of the people around us. I shuddered at what they might think. And who could blame them? I was talking to the Mormon erotica writer who used to be my girlfriend. A refrain from my youth repeated in my brain. *Remember who you are and what you stand for.* If I had any sense of decorum, I told myself, I'd end this conversation, congratulate the newlyweds, and find Miss Right by the punchbowl. Instead, I heard myself say, "Can we get out of here?"

Sadie stared back at me, looking as shocked as I felt.

"We could go to Starbucks," I added.

Her dimples reappeared. "Sure."

My heart still pounding, I ushered her out of the building and across the parking lot, anxious to be off the premises. Her heels clicked along the pavement as we walked. I noticed that she was a couple of inches shorter than me, just the right height to lay her head on my shoulder. My mind flashed back to the first time we slow danced.

"Sister Gordon." Ginger Haas ran after us, hiking the skirt of her yellow bridesmaid's gown.

"Oops! I promised this girl a book," said Sadie. "There's one on my backseat."

Shifting my weight from one foot to the other, I kept a lookout for nosey church members while Sadie autographed her novel. Thankfully, none wandered by.

"Starbucks is just up the street," I said, once my bishop's youngest daughter had left with her signed copy of *Laying on of Hands.* "Follow me?" I pointed to my Prius. "Same model as yours."

As I drove I remembered that Sunday School story about a job interview for drivers on a dangerous route. The first applicant said he could drive clear to the edge of the road. The second said he could drive partially over the edge. The third said he stayed as far from the edge as possible. Shaking my head as I pulled into a parking space, I felt myself drifting toward the edge.

But once safe inside the establishment where my sister claimed no decent woman could be found, my anxiety eased. I bought us a decaf coffee and a hot chocolate and then showed Sadie to my usual table.

She took a drink of her decaf. "Remember that pompous lecture you gave me when I ordered the Dr. Pepper?"

"I remember you threw it in my face."

"I was so mad at you."

"*You* were mad at *me*?"

"I also recall how we made up."

I blushed and swigged my chocolate.

Sadie used her napkin to dab the edge of my mouth. "Whipped cream," she explained.

"I heard you got divorced. How come?" I asked.

"You still don't beat around the bush."

"Nope."

"Still a perfect Mormon, Jim?"

"Nope again. I'm a divorced single dad."

"How many kids?"

"I have a fourteen-year-old daughter, Julia."

Sadie grinned. "Oh my, a teenaged girl."

"Don't get me started."

"Still a right-winger?"

"Nope. In fact, my sister claims I'm an eco-fascist."

She ran a slender finger around the rim of her cup. "Excellent. Still a computer nerd?"

"Freelance nerd. I design mobile apps. Still cheat at Scrabble, Sadie?"

"I've never cheated at Scrabble, Maxwell. You still think a

Woody Allen movie qualifies as porn?"

"I liked *Manhattan Murder Mystery.*"

"How about *Vicky Cristina Barcelona?*"

"Haven't seen it. Let's move on to music. Still a fan of Men Without Hats?"

Sadie burst out laughing, and in a manner so infectious it drew smiles from the people around us.

After a long breath, she answered, "I'm a Tony Bennett, Michael Bublé kind of person these days."

"Why'd you get divorced, Sadie?"

"We were both Mormons at the time and only married because we were desperate to have sex. After that, there was nothing to talk about." Her neckline slipped sideways to reveal her bra strap. It was silky and beige like her dress.

"No back and forth over politics? Woody Allen?"

"He only watched sports."

"I'm sorry."

"Don't be. The sex was fantastic. We even kept it up after the divorce."

My lips parted.

"But now he's remarried. She models lingerie."

All of a sudden I started sweating. I loosened my tie and undid my top button. "Kids?" I half-gasped.

"No. No kids." Sadie leaned against the booth and the silky strap disappeared. "And I'm married to my work."

"You don't date?"

She shook her head. "You remember how much I hated those church mix and mingles."

"But now you don't go to them."

"Yeah, I do. Only with alcohol. And it does nothing to dull the pain."

I laughed.

"Besides, I'm still hopelessly attracted to Mormon men."

"Really?" My pulse rose.

She shrugged. "At least I can write them into erotic scenes."

My cheeks burning, I grabbed for my cup and nearly knocked it over.

"What's your story, Jim?"

I took a long sip of chocolate, collecting myself as I swallowed. "After grad school I moved back here and met a pretty girl I liked. We lasted three years."

"A pretty girl you *liked*? I'm surprised it lasted three years."

"She wouldn't let me touch her."

Sadie stared at me. In this light her eyes looked more green than brown. "How'd Julia happen?"

"Whitney only let me violate her during ovulation. That's what she called it, *violation*."

"Sounds like she needed professional help."

"She thought I was the one who needed help. Said I had a sex addiction. Kept prodding me to talk to the bishop."

"Did you?"

All of a sudden I found myself making a conscientious effort not to look at her breasts. "Did I what? Have a sex addiction?"

"No." She laughed and briefly squeezed my arm, sending a shiver of excitement through to my bones. "Did you talk to your bishop?"

"Sure. A couple of them, in fact. They sympathized with my situation, but couldn't offer any advice other than to be patient with her."

"What about Whitney? Did you ask her what she wanted in bed?"

"Gosh, yes. I even searched online for ideas. When I suggested some she went ballistic, claimed I was demanding she perform unnatural acts."

Sadie set down her coffee cup and in a raised voice said, "For heaven's sake, there's nothing wrong with oral sex."

The couple at the next booth smiled our way. I realized that someday I was going to have to reconstruct this conversation in order to understand just how we got to this point.

"Actually, I never asked for … that."

"What then?"

I blushed again and mumbled, "Her on top."

Sadie rolled her eyes and took my hands in hers. "Jim, you're a handsome, sexy man, and funny as hell. There are plenty of Mormon women who like sex. I know. I hear from them."

I struggled to form a reply, but all I could think about was how much I wanted to kiss her.

"Thanks for the coffee." She stood up.

I jumped to my feet. "Can we do this again? I'll come to San Francisco."

Sadie blinked. "I guess."

I checked the calendar on my phone. Julia was with me this weekend, but she had a sleepover. "Friday night?"

"I'm sorry, I'm committed to an ex-Mormon party in the City."

"Next weekend then?"

"Maybe. Message me."

I drove home, went straight to my computer, and sent Sadie a Facebook message about next weekend. After that I downloaded *Laying on of Hands* onto my Kindle.

5

My mobile woke me from a deep sleep. Eyes shut, I groped for it on my nightstand. "Hullo."

"Dad, are you dating Sadie Gordon?"

I opened my eyes. My Kindle was on the pillow next to me. "What?"

"People overheard you asking her to Starbucks last night."

I dropped the phone. From somewhere on the bed, Julia cried, "Dad, are you there?" I fumbled in the sheets to find the thing.

"Honey, it wasn't a date."

"Will you get me a signed copy of her book?"

"I will not."

"Dad, it's not that bad."

"You've read it?"

"All the girls have."

"I'll call you back, kiddo."

My clock said nine fifty, meaning I'd gotten three hours sleep, half of it consumed by Mom lamenting that I hadn't kissed Sadie, the other half filled with dreams that I had. I'd finished the book. The writing was as enchanting as the author herself. Also, Julia was right. It wasn't that bad. There was plenty of sex, all right, but only within the bonds of marriage or the in realm of fantasy. And none of the content was graphic enough to be considered erotica. Not to a mainstream audience, anyway. But then my desire to kiss the author had enhanced my particular reading experience. Had she really meant what she'd said last night? That she was only attracted to Mormon men? I climbed out of bed and took a cold shower.

At church the usual busybodies inquired after my love life and I got a few winks from the guys in High Priests Group. Those I could handle. But the dagger glares from Kellie meant certain doom for our weekly Sunday dinner. Also the three hours of shut-eye I'd gotten left me ill prepared to make it through three hours of church. I did my best to stay focused through Sacrament Meeting but slipped off to sleep toward the end of Sunday School, despite the efforts of Sister Hawkins whose lessons were always interesting. I rallied during Priesthood, at first thanks to some entertaining discussion, later by shuffling the scriptures on my app. That was, until a passage in Acts, Peter preaching repentance to the Israelites, lit up my screen. Suddenly uncomfortable, I shut off my phone and spent the remaining minutes mulling over how to explain last night to Kellie. Problem was, I couldn't even explain it to myself.

Kellie lived on the corner of a small cul-de-sac. There were three other houses on the street, all inhabited by families of sketchy religious affiliations, an environment that prompted my sister to refer to her neighborhood as "the world."

I parked in her drive, undid my tie, and tossed it on the backseat. Trudging to the door, I rang the bell and waited as ominous footsteps approached. To my momentary relief, they belonged to my brother-in-law, Craig. I admired my brother-in-law. He was both devout and nonjudgmental. Like me, I wanted to think, only without the male pattern baldness. Not only had he shed his tie, he'd also managed to change into a tee shirt and sweat pants. I shook his hand hello and then stepped inside to see my sister, clad in her church dress and bedroom slippers, motioning me toward her kitchen. Sighing, I filed obediently after her, through the living and then the dining room, stopping briefly at the door to the family room where my three nephews, also dressed in tees and sweats, were strewn like driftwood in front of a football game.

"Hi guys."

"'Lo, Uncle Jim," they called in unison, their eyes glued to the oversized flat screen.

Smiling sadly, I went to face Kellie. As always, the kitchen table was set for six and the unmistakable aroma of her chicken and broccoli casserole filled the air. My stomach growled.

"You're dating an anti-Mormon?" She lodged a hand on her hip.

"She's not an anti-Mormon and we're not dating. She's an old friend."

"An old girlfriend."

"We broke up years ago."

"She quit the church, wrote a dirty book, and speaks out against our stand on traditional marriage."

"You left out that she drives a Prius."

Kellie pursed her lips. "You were going to reintroduce yourself to Lorraine, not drink coffee with an anti-Mormon."

"Hot chocolate, not coffee."

"In one of their cups."

"Yes."

My sister made no return to the subject during dinner, probably because the boys were at the table with us. With that in mind, I insisted on helping my nephews clear the plates after the meal. Then I deftly avoided Kellie's invitation to sit with her and Craig in the living room.

"I'd like to, sis, but I'm beat. I didn't get much sleep last night."

Her eyes narrowed into slits. "Oh, *really*? Why not, Jim?"

Ignoring her question, I shook Craig's hand goodbye, and made a speedy exit to my car.

On the drive home my mind was consumed with Sadie. Her adorable dimples, the sexy curves of her silky beige dress, the occasional glimpse of her bra strap. The way she'd made me laugh, how she'd drawn me out on the subject of my failed marriage, something my last three bishops hadn't been able to do. For crying out loud, did we really talk about oral sex? After all these years, how had this woman managed to unlock me?

I got to the house and first thing opened my laptop on the kitchen counter. I checked my Facebook messages for a response from Sadie. No reply. It was almost twenty-four hours since I'd written to ask when I could see her again. What was the hold-up? Was she too busy? I clicked on her wall. Her profile picture showed her in a little black dress holding a glass of wine. Her eyes gazed back at me, searing clear through to my heart. Should I send another message? I didn't want to sound desperate. But then, I didn't have to bring up seeing her. I could just tell her how much I liked her book. Her book that I'd stayed up all night reading. Talk about sounding desperate. I closed my laptop and went to my bedroom to change into my pajamas. Fatigue wore heavily upon me. I was fading fast, so fast that I might not even make it another fifteen minutes to the start of the evening news. I picked up my phone, stretched out on my bed, and brought up the Scripture Mastery app. The verses from Acts were still on the screen.

Repent ye therefore, and be converted, that your sins may be blotted out, when the times of refreshing shall come from the presence of the Lord.

I turned off my phone without finishing the passage. For some reason I felt defensive, kind of like when Bishop Haas nagged me about my absence from the single adult activities. But why? I didn't need to repent. For the past twelve years my cruise control had been set under the speed limit and I had stayed dead center on the straight and narrow. Nowhere near the edge.

Could the Spirit be warning that my reconnection with Sadie threatened to throw me off course? My head sank deeper into the pillow. Not possible, I told myself. Sadie and I were just old friends. With our core beliefs so different, how could we ever be more than that? Despite my initial infatuation, we'd end up like Marcia and me. Of course, in the future I'd need to keep my eyes off of her bra strap and steer clear of subjects like oral sex.

I propped up on the bed, found the TV remote, and switched on the evening news. An offshore storm had sent record-breaking surf onto San Francisco's Ocean Beach. This made me think of Sadie. I reached for my phone and logged onto Facebook. She still hadn't responded to my message. My eyes slid shut.

Maybe I'd been right in the first place. This was my mother's idea of a joke.

The Unabridged Journal of Julia Camilla Maxwell
Sunday, October 13
9:10 p.m.

The most bizarro Sabbath ever. And it wasn't Heavenly Father's fault. It was Dad's fault for flirting. Yes, **FLIRTING** at a Mormon wedding reception last night. With Sadie Gordon, no less, the author of that sexy novel that half the women at church have read but none will admit to owning. First thing in the foyer this morning the ward members circled like sharks.

"Did they really go to Starbucks?" "What time did he get home last night?" "Does he know how fast she is?" "Has he read her book?" "Does your dad drink coffee now?" Oh, and my favorite: "What happened to him and Lorraine Grace?"

Excuse me. Lorraine who? This is my dad we're talking about. My nerdy, anti-social dad who thinks thin crust pizza is haute cuisine and splurging means paying full price at Target. My dad who blushes during feminine product commercials and looks away when he walks past the window at Victoria's Secret. Up until now his only "passion" has been designing dorky computer apps. Now there are TWO women in his life and one of them writes erotica?

Crazy as it sounds there is some truth to it. When I called and asked him about Sadie I could feel Dad turning red from clear across town. He couldn't wait to hang up and promised to call me back but hasn't. Not that I mind, since I've still no good excuse for not meeting with Bishop Franklin.

At least the girls my age are cool—especially if I can get them signed copies of Sadie's book. The boys are being jerks, but then what else is new? Mormon guys are definitely not my thing. My taste is decidedly more worldly. As in 4th period. Yum! Maybe I take after Dad.

The mere mention of Sadie Gordon has driven my already mental mother into this catatonic state, a scary calm that surely precedes an eruption the size of Vesuvius. When I pray to Heavenly

Father tonight my first order of business will be to thank Him for inspiring me to start this secret journal. Next up will be to ask that I might be as far away as possible when my mother finally and predictably blows her top.

6

Days passed and I followed Sadie's Facebook posts. On the one hand, her irreverence and her decided disrespect for the church reminded me of how unsuited we were for each other. On the other hand, her frankness along with her adorable dimples kept luring me back to her wall. Many of her posts were attached to articles critical of church policy, sites that poked fun at LDS culture, or her own blog, a sort of Mormon version of the *Kama Sutra*. But not everything she shared was church related. On Tuesday she put up a quote from Albert Camus about friendship and tagged a dozen or so people. I wasn't among them. Later that day she posted a funny clip from a late night talk show, also a *San Francisco Chronicle* article about the homeless. But she didn't reply to my message.

When Wednesday afternoon rolled around and I still hadn't heard from her, my resentment kicked in. All of this "sitting by the phone" was taking a toll on my ego, and I felt like a fool for staying up all night to finish her book. At this point, I told myself, it didn't matter if she wrote back. Okay, so Sadie had a nice figure and a pretty face and she managed to make me laugh. But she'd made me wait too long. I was a busy man. I could hardly drop everything and go all the way to San Francisco. Besides, she could never be more than a friend. Meanwhile, I knew plenty of eligible Mormon women here in San Jose. Not that I wanted to date any of them. But I could, and without any fear of our conversations drifting toward sex. My ego repaired, I went to pick Julia up at school.

She wore a long face when she climbed in the car, was distant on the drive home, and then spent the remainder of the afternoon at the kitchen table with her homework, barely touching the milk and Oreos I'd set out for her. I wondered if a trip to the local pizza joint might lighten her mood, and perhaps entice her to unload whatever it was that had been bothering her lately.

"What's on your mind, kiddo?" I asked after the waitress had brought our drinks.

"I'm a little worried." She fiddled with the straw in her root beer. "It's Mom. I think she may be going bonkers."

"What now?" I cleared my throat and then rephrased the question. "I mean, why do you think your mother might be going crazy?"

"She had this mythic meltdown after she heard about you and Sadie going to Starbucks on Saturday."

I nodded. "In time, when nothing comes of it, I'm sure your mother will be herself again."

"You know she took your break-up pretty hard."

"Yeah," I said softly. "It was harder on her because I was the one who filed for divorce."

"She thought you'd come back to her."

"In the beginning, she believed that, I know," I replied. Although why she'd wanted me back remained a mystery to me.

"Actually, she still believes that."

"Why on earth would she think such a thing?"

"Well, you know how you never date."

"Uh-huh," I mumbled, already uncomfortable with where this father-daughter conversation was heading.

"Mom assumes that the reason you don't date is because you've never gotten over her."

The waitress returned with our twelve-inch thin crust pepperoni. Julia took the first slice and set it on her plate without taking a bite.

"How do you know this?" I asked.

"Because she talks to me about it, Dad. She wants to know if you ask about her. On the way to seminary this morning she told me to be sure to tell you she's free for dinner Friday night."

"Friday night?"

"I've got that sleepover. The two of you could party."

I stared back at her in dumbfounded silence.

"See what I mean? Bonkers, right, Dad?"

The restaurant was empty except for a party of three across the room. Most of the place's business was in deliveries. Precisely why I liked to come here. "Why haven't you told me about this?"

She frowned. "I didn't want to talk about it, to her or you."

I reached over and squeezed her hand. Neither of us had begun to eat.

"I understand, honey. I'm just a little shocked. I left your mother twelve years ago." I helped myself to a slice. "I've never even hinted at coming back to her."

"Yeah, I know. But she thinks the two of you are still married."

"For crying out loud, your mother and I are divorced." I took a bite and then angrily chewed and swallowed.

"I know. But in a court, right, Dad?"

"Yes, of course in a court."

"But not in the temple?"

"The court is what counts. Look, I'm sorry you've had to deal with this, honey. I will talk to her."

"Thanks." She took a bite of her own and gave it time to begin digesting before asking, "Dad, do we believe in polygamy?"

"Absolutely not," I replied, loudly enough to draw the attention of the party of three.

"But you could get married in the temple and still stay married to Mom, right?"

"Julia, once and for all, your mother and I are divorced."

"But not in the temple."

I drew a breath. "We were divorced by a judge."

"Mom doesn't care about the judge."

"Is your mother telling you that I'm still married to her?"

Julia shook her head as she chewed. "Not exactly. Mom knows you're divorced down here, but in heaven, she thinks she gets you back. Do you believe that, Dad?"

Smiling, I helped myself to another slice. "I will continue this conversation with your mother."

"Mom also says that the three of us are sealed for eternity.

Sorry, Dad, but I know that's not happening. I love you and Mom, but separately. I'd go nuts if I had to be with both of you at the same time, even for a few—"

I issued a mirthless laugh. "I'm sure Heavenly Father will grant you permission to disown each of us."

"Okay, but can a man be married to more than one woman in the temple?"

"Technically, yes," I admitted.

"So it *is* true that when you die, you're supposed to have hundreds of wives and an entire planet to populate?"

"Where did you hear that?"

"In Young Women's."

"From Sister Gleener?"

"No. Bishop Franklin. He drops in to speak to us most Sundays."

Wiping my hands on my napkin, I paused to consider this information. Sounded like this Franklin was even more over-the-top than Whitney. "Julia, is that why you don't want to meet with Bishop Franklin? Because you don't like his opinions?"

She frowned and stared at her plate. "I guess so."

"It's okay not to agree with him, kiddo. You know that, right?"

Nodding, she met my eyes. "But do Mormons really think that they're going to have their own planets?"

"Technically that is still the doctrine." I smiled. "But I certainly do not see such a scenario *anywhere* in my future."

"This polygamy in heaven notion is pretty bizarre. Not to mention insulting to women. What does Sadie Gordon think about it?"

The mention of Sadie made my heart race. "I don't know," I replied, remembering the link Sadie'd posted on Facebook yesterday, the one about Joseph Smith's plural wives.

"You never talked about it when you were dating? Or the other night at Starbucks?"

The other night at Starbucks we'd talked about oral sex. "That would hardly be a subject for mixed company," I insisted.

"Dad, you're turning red."

"I'm not … the pepperoni's a little spicy, that's all." I gave her hand another squeeze. "Look, everything will work out in heaven. That's why it's heaven."

Julia stared back at me, unconvinced. I knew I was oversimplifying, but I also knew that obsessing over sticky points of doctrine could destroy a person's testimony. I didn't want to see her go down that road. "I just don't think you should worry about it, kiddo."

"Sure, Dad."

I offered her the last slice of pizza. She took it.

"Say, Dad. Who is Lorraine Grace?"

My cheeks burned. "Why do you ask?"

"People are saying you're an item."

I started to explain and then thought better of it. "Julia, do you need help with your Algebra?"

"Nope. I've got that covered, Dad."

That night I dreamt that Mom and I were in the old Chevy, sitting in traffic, in the stifling heat.

"I want to be at the beach," I said.

The car levitated and we were flying over the clogged streets to the ocean. I bounced in my seat. "Really? Can we?"

Mom turned to me. In the waning golden and pink light she had never looked younger, or more beautiful. "You want something in life, Jimmy, you go for it," she said, and nodded at the shore below us.

I jumped out of the car, floated gently onto the sand, and rushed to the water.

The Unabridged Journal of Julia Camilla Maxwell
Wednesday, October 16
9:10 p.m.

Update: both my parents are bonkers.

Mom erupted last night. Went on about the harlots who are after her eternal husband. Called Sadie all kinds of names and went off on this Lorraine Grace person, a woman she's only seen from a distance but insists is a "cafeteria Mormon who dresses immodestly." Of course Mom says the same thing about Aunt Kellie, Marie Osmond, and Ann Romney.

Meanwhile, tonight Dad went Black Ops, dodging my questions and turning red. He doesn't get how upset Mom is and was a total spaz at explaining polygamy. But then, since he's still married to Mom in the temple and maybe seeing two other women on the side, I suppose the subjects are sticky ones for him right now. At least he's stopped giving me sideways looks.

Which brings me to the one sliver of silver lining. My bonkers dad's new "playboy status" has completely distracted him from worrying about mine. Plus all the gossip swirling around has made my bonkers mom hurry the both of us out of the building right after church. Before I can meet with Bishop Franklin. Sweet!

7

Thursday morning I had just left Julia at early morning seminary and was contemplating my latest visitation from Mom when the phone rang. Kellie. I hit accept on my car dashboard.

"Sis."

"Jimmy, can you talk?"

"Sure. I just dropped off Julia."

"Great, because I have a brilliant idea."

"What now?" I turned onto Almaden Expressway.

"Why don't I invite both you and Lorraine Grace for dinner tomorrow night?"

"Wouldn't that be a bit obvious?" I rolled my eyes, thinking of last night's conversation with Julia. "Also, it's kind of short notice. I'm awfully busy these days."

"Have you looked in the mirror lately? Seen that receding hairline of yours? You're not exactly in a position to play hard to get."

I coughed and then cleared my throat. "Gee, thanks, sis. You're all heart."

"I'm just saying that at your age, if you want something, you go for it."

Letting her words hang in the air for several seconds, I marveled at how she'd echoed Mom in last night's dream—only without the self-abandon, joie de vivre, and magic flying car. But then, what more could I expect at my age?

"All right, Kel. But it can't be a date."

"Oh, no," she insisted. "Just a friendly dinner."

"Okay."

"Super. I'll contact Lorraine and let you know her reply."

"Thank you." I stopped behind a long line of cars at Blossom Hill Road. I could see that it was going to take two traffic signal cycles to get through the intersection.

"I take it you're on your way to Starbucks?" Kellie asked.

"I'm working from home today."

"Excellent."

"Bye, sis."

Later that morning a text came in from Kellie: *Lorraine's a yes! Tomorrow 6:00.* That afternoon I got a friend request from Lorraine. I accepted and sent a message saying that I looked forward to a friendly dinner. She replied with a smiley face.

I ventured over to her wall. Her profile picture showed her in front of the Missionary Training Center, her arm about a gangly missionary, presumably her son. She didn't have Sadie's sexy curves and adorable dimples, but Lorraine looked very becoming in her trim navy suit and heels. Her eyes were warm and her smile gentle, if a little sad, not unlike my own. First glance, she looked like the perfect non-date for me.

A quick scroll of her recent posts confirmed my impression. There was a link to a talk from an LDS General Conference, a video recipe for cherry-chocolate chews, a picture of her on the beach with a towel draped across the bottom portion of her one-piece, and a reply to a Facebook meme asking for her favorite books. Her list included *Charlotte's Web, The Screwtape Letters,* a couple of Tom Clancy titles, the *Twilight* series, and a biography of Mitt Romney.

I liked that *Laying on of Hands* wasn't on her list. I also liked that she'd taken the courtesy to swiftly return my message. Beyond that, her wall failed to arouse any excitement. I suppose even then part of me knew that this set-up was never going to work. But I smiled and went along anyway, sort of like on my honeymoon.

8

Friday morning I awoke from a dreamless sleep. Speculating that meant Mom approved of my non-date with Lorraine, and now logically convinced that I was on the right track, I buried myself in work until it was time to pick up Julia.

But on the drive to Almaden Valley, Sadie tugged on my heart again. Why hadn't she returned my message? Maybe she didn't get it. Or maybe she was too busy. Busy doing what, I wondered, as I stopped in front of the school. Then Julia ran straight for my car, inspiring the first smile of my day.

"Do you need to go by Mom's house for your sleepover clothes?" I asked as she buckled herself in.

"Nope. They're in my backpack."

"Then let's go for a treat. You choose where."

We ended up on a bench in front of the frozen yogurt shop with a couple of soft serve cones.

"So, kiddo, what's on the agenda at tonight's sleepover?"

"Girl talk," she replied and ran her tongue around her chocolate and vanilla swirl.

"Hmm, sounds more like 'boy talk.'"

She giggled. "That, too."

I waited. When she didn't elaborate, I tried to think of a diplomatic way to expand the topic. Instead, she changed the subject.

"Mom reminded me to tell you she's free for dinner tonight."

"And now you have." I realized I was going to have to talk to Whitney, and sooner rather than later. But the wording, that was always the tricky part. She could be so touchy.

"What are you doing tonight, Dad?"

"I'm going to Aunt Kellie's for dinner."

"On Friday? Is it a special occasion?"

"Not really, no." Catching her stare in my peripheral vision, I explained, "Aunt Kellie's invited an old friend over."

Julia jumped in with, "Is it Sadie?"

"No, this is another old friend, a nice Mormon woman."

"Are you saying Sadie isn't nice?"

"*No*, of course not." Although I was still annoyed that I hadn't heard back from her.

"Sadie is also a Mormon," Julia added.

"True, but she's no longer active in the church. The woman coming to dinner tonight is."

"Is it Lorraine Grace, Dad?"

"Yes," I replied in a succinct tone I hoped would put an end to the subject.

"So you *are* an item."

"No. And this is not a date. Just a friendly dinner." I licked my vanilla level with the cone. Julia's frozen yogurt, I noticed, had begun dripping onto her paper napkin.

"You seem to be going on a lot of non-dates these days, Dad."

I exhaled. "Do you plan on finishing that? Or are you just going to let it melt all over your hand?"

She cut me a knowing look, at once revealing a terrifying dichotomy. As a parent, I was totally blind to what was going on in my kid's head. She, on the other hand, had high-powered laser vision into mine. I scowled, pulled out my mobile and hit shuffle on the Scripture Mastery app.

"First Corinthians fifteen, verses forty through forty-two."

Julia made a face. "Dad, I told you we aren't even close to first Corinthians yet."

"Here's a hint. *Degrees of Glory.*"

"Why can't I just read the New Testament books in order? Brother Price says that's most important."

"It *is* most important, of course, but there's nothing wrong with skipping ahead." I held up my hand in a halting gesture. "There are also celestial bodies, and bodies terrestrial; but the glory of the celestial is one, and—"

"Oh, I get it," she interrupted. "This is the one about how

everything will work out in heaven."

My arm fell to my side. "Let's go to the car."

I dropped Julia at her sleepover and went home to shave, shower, and change into the navy slacks and yellow polo I'd selected to wear to the friendly dinner at Kellie's. I checked myself out in the mirror. My sister was right. With my paunch and disappearing hairline, I was in no position to play hard to get. But I looked like a nice enough Mormon guy, dressed just right for a non-date with a nice enough Mormon woman. Layer on my zippered golf jacket and the look would be complete.

By then it was only four thirty. I crossed the hall to my office and opened my laptop on the desk. First I checked my email. Two new messages. An ad from Target and an investment opportunity with somebody in Nigeria. I surfed over to the *New York Times.* There was nothing new to report and my online subscription didn't include the crossword puzzle. The clock on my laptop read four forty-one. I went back to my mailbox. No new messages. I opened the ad from Target and scrolled through the sale on men's and then women's clothing. One of the models resembled Sadie. I closed the ad and clicked on my games where I lost one and then another round of solitaire. Exhaling, I leaned back in my chair and rubbed my eyes. Then I gave in and logged onto Facebook. As fate would have it, a post from Sadie was at the top of my feed.

Can somebody give me a lift home from the ex-Mormon party at the Seagull Bar tonight?

I scrolled through the comments. Twenty-four replies, mostly from people using fake identities. A woman named "X-Molly" wrote, *You bet,* and a character named "Breed M. Young" offered to buy her a martini. Then a new comment popped up from somebody named Wally T: *Babe, I'd kill to take you home!*

My body tensed. Who the heck was he? I clicked on Wally's profile. His relationship status said "single" and he was interested in "women." His picture showed him sitting poolside in a lawn chair. He looked like a jerk.

Back on Sadie's wall, five more had commented, all of them guys, all of them wanting to take her home. My palms began to sweat.

I logged off the computer and ran to the bedroom for my wallet and keys. Then on the way to the closet for my golf jacket, I caught sight of myself in the mirror. Navy khakis and a dorky yellow polo. Cringing, I left the coat behind, ran out the door, jumped in my car, and sped to the mall.

The saleslady at Nordstrom couldn't have been more than thirty years old. She greeted me the minute I arrived in Menswear.

"I need to look ... " I froze, terrified of what I was about to say. "Attractive."

She grinned. "Do you have a date?"

"Yes," I replied evenly. "I'm afraid that I do."

She helped me find a black designer tee shirt, some jeans that managed to contain my girth, and a black lightweight wool sports coat. I had her cut the tags and handed over my credit card. She came back for my signature. The total read $753.97. I blinked and then signed.

Surprisingly light traffic took me quickly through Silicon Valley and then flying past San Mateo County's oak-laden hills. When I got to the City, my GPS directed me to a dive in the Outer Richmond. Gazing up at the neon seagull perched on an oversized martini glass, I wondered briefly if I'd gone mad.

It wasn't as though I'd never been to a bar. In fact, I'd been to several. Corporate-sponsored happy hours, usually at high-end establishments with a deferential wait staff, quiet background music, and a well-heeled clientele. I generally nursed a ginger ale, even though I didn't particularly care for the stuff. But it seemed less conspicuous than a glass of ice water or, even worse, nothing at all. Not that I minded being seen without a drink. But my abstinence always seemed to create anxiety for the handful of colleagues who wrongly assumed I was judging them. "I'm really *not* much of a drinker, Jim," he or she might explain before half-heartedly declining the server's offer for a refill.

Only, as I stood here on this foggy block in the Outer Richmond, staring at the blinking Bud-Lite sign in the bar window, I could tell I was about to enter uncharted territory. Nevertheless, I knew I had to go for it.

The Seagull was noisy and packed. I spotted a man at the bar in a tee shirt that read *Small Hands—Huge Testimony.*

"You look like you might be an ex-Mormon," a fresh-faced woman said. She wore the top of an LDS temple garment with a red bra underneath. Some sort of black spandex contraption barely covered the bottom half of her essentials.

"Oh, yeah? What makes you think that?" I asked, struggling to keep my eyes level with her face.

Her smile broadened. "We're in the back. Buy yourself a drink and join us."

I thanked her and, realizing at once that I posed no threat to anyone's enjoyment, I skipped the ginger ale, and forced my way through the crowd to the backroom. Some kids that I hoped the bartender had carded were performing a drunken parody of the BYU Fight Song:

Rise and shout, we're here to make out; we're on the road to Provo Canyon.

Beyond them a group gathered who, minus their cocktails, could have passed for members of my ward Priesthood and Relief Society. Marginally relieved to see them, I was about to ask if they'd seen Sadie when my mobile vibrated. Kellie. I stared at the screen, briefly imagining our conversation. *Kel, can you speak up? The drunks in this bar are really noisy.* As her call went to voicemail, the refrain from my youth repeated in my brain. *Remember who you are and what you stand for.* Honestly, what on earth was I doing here? If I had any sense of decorum, I'd leave immediately, call my sister, and make my excuses. Pretty much anything other than the truth would do.

Returning my phone to my pocket, I looked around for the closest exit. I had just spotted it when Sadie appeared. She was in a skimpy green dress, high heels, and holding a martini, just like a looker in a high-end liquor ad. Her hazel eyes widened.

"Jim. You're so handsome."

My heart pounded. "You're gorgeous."

She kissed the edge of my mouth and then jumped away, spilling part of her drink in the process. "I'm so sorry."

"I'm not."

Sadie set down her glass. "I should never drink around attractive men who are off limits."

"Why am I off limits?"

"What are you doing at an ex-Mormon party?"

"Why didn't you return my message?" I felt myself getting worked up. It was *her* fault I was at an ex-Mormon party.

"I was going to. I just … got busy."

"Busy doing what?" There was an edge to my voice I wished wasn't there.

Her gaze hardened. "Jim, it was fun running into you the other night. But why would you want to take things any further?"

I looked back at the High Priests Group. The guy in the navy polo resembled Wally T. But then so did the business suit with the wineglass. I scowled and pointed at her martini. "Who bought you that drink?" Again, the edge.

She balked and then picked up her glass and downed what was left in it. "Who cares?"

"I care. And who's Wally T?"

She glared back at me, a little woozy, clearly exasperated, and sexy as hell. "Maxwell, why are you here?"

"To see you."

"Don't you get that I'm never going back to the church?"

I glanced around. Temple Garment Girl was throwing back shots with Huge Testimony, and the drunken troubadours had moved on to Primary songs.

"Oh … I think I get that."

I turned back to Sadie. The high heels had brought her mouth up level with mine. Her lips were pink and moist and slightly parted. I stepped forward and kissed them, pulling her close in my arms. She melted against me, just like in college. Then I took her face in my hands and looked into her eyes. "Can we get out of here?"

"Sure."

Slipping my arm around her waist, I led her out the nearest exit and to my car; she wobbled a bit along the way. We drove down to Ocean Beach, our eyes forward, neither of us speaking. The minute I parked, we started kissing, struggling to unhook our seatbelts.

"This is wrong," Sadie breathed. "I'm married to my work."

"Are you writing a sequel?"

"Yes."

My lips trailed up her neck. "Think of me as research," I whispered, and silenced her response with more deep, moist kisses. We made out in the front seat like a couple of teenagers, lingering as long as we could until urgency began pushing us to the next step. Sadie pulled away and I straightened in my seat. For a couple of awkward seconds we sat staring at each other, both of us breathless, and suddenly shy.

"Like to go for a walk?" I asked.

She nodded yes.

Wrapped together in a blanket from my trunk, we strolled barefoot along the cool sand, the occasional fire pit lighting our way, our conversation flowing to and fro as easily as the surf.

I asked her if she went to ex-Mormon parties often. She said no, called them "LDS mix and mingles with cocktails," and again joked that the alcohol did nothing to dull the pain. She asked me if I went to many wedding receptions. I also replied in the negative, and went on to confess that when I did I invariably felt like I needed one of those cocktails. Laughing over our shared foibles, we rediscovered the reasons we had become a couple in the first place. Amazingly, it seemed that time had only reinforced our commonality. Sadie had definitely softened. She was still feisty in her opinions, but not to the point of hurling a soft drink. And thank heaven I'd lightened up. Honestly, had I really blown up over a measly Dr. Pepper? Now we were just two loners who liked working at home, hated mixing and mingling, got the same jokes, and, up until tonight, rarely did anything unlikely. Wrapped together in the blanket, the moon shimmering overhead, what we shared seemed as vast and powerful as the ocean that crashed onto the shore before us. True, I was under the influence of nostalgia, paired with a healthy dose of infatuation. But it was also true that Sadie had unlocked a door deep in my heart, and the feelings spilling through it were real, just as they had been in college.

As night turned to morning, I took her home to her place in the Inner Sunset. We exchanged drowsy kisses on the sofa, where she fell asleep in my arms.

I knew the memory of that night would be forever etched in my brain, poised to surface at will, and with intense clarity. Depending on how things played out, it promised to inspire my deepest joy, or my most painful longing. But during those final moments we spent together, with all reservations shoved to the back of my mind, I simply lay awake holding her, awash in the blissful sensation of being with a woman who wanted me.

9

Saturday morning I cruised down the peninsula, still riding my wave of bliss. I made it to San Jose just in time to pick up Julia from her sleepover.

"Dad, what are you wearing?" she asked as we pulled away from her friend's house.

"New clothes."

Julia fingered the sleeve of my sport coat.

"I wanted to look nice for my date last night," I blurted out, smiling.

"You said it wasn't going to be a date."

"It wasn't." My hand wavered above the steering wheel.

"Why'd you just call it that, then?"

"I didn't mean date as in *date*, I meant last night's friendly dinner."

"So how come you're still wearing last night's friendly dinner clothes this morning?"

"I'm not *still* wearing them. I overslept and threw them on to come get you."

This was precisely the kind of sloppy lie I used to pull on Mom when I was a teenager. The kind she never fell for.

"Dad, you're turning red."

"It's just too warm in here." I rolled down my window, welcoming the distraction of street sounds.

Julia continued to stare at me. "Last night's dinner must have gotten *really* friendly."

I started to correct her and then shrugged. There was no need for me to explain myself to my daughter. After all, it wasn't like I'd had sex. I'd just spent the night ... only with Sadie, not Lorraine. I stifled a snicker.

"Oh, by the way," Julia added. "Aunt Kellie texted me this morning. She wants you to call her."

"I imagine she does."

"Think she wants to talk to you about last night, Dad?"

"She might."

Back at my house, I helped Julia get started on her science project and then went to my master suite to shower and change. Even after bathing, Sadie's scent still seemed to linger on my skin. I glanced out my bedroom window into the garden. It looked more vivid and colorful than it had when I'd left it and, despite the awkward phone call I was about to make, made me feel extraordinarily happy. I switched on my mobile phone. The screen lit up to show I had four voicemails from Kellie and one from Marcia. I grinned. My best friend, Marcia. She was probably the only person I could talk to about Sadie right now. But first I had to deal with Kellie.

"Dad, can you help me?" Julia called.

I went to the dining room to see her holding up a coil of insulated wire. A "D" battery, modeling clay, and sundry small household items were splayed across the table waiting to be assembled into an electrical motor.

"What do you need, kiddo?"

"The hobby knife so I can cut the insulation off the ends of the wire."

"You mean *I* need the hobby knife so *I* can cut the insulation."

She rolled her eyes. "Dad, I'm old enough to use a knife. In school they even let me use pointy scissors."

"Humor me, then."

I found the knife in my kitchen tool drawer, performed the task, and gave her shoulder a squeeze. Then I walked out my back door into the brilliant fall day and dialed my sister.

The phone rang four times before she finally picked up. I envisioned her staring at my ID on her screen through all of them.

"Hello, Jim."

"Sis, hi." I paced away from the house. "I'm sorry about last night."

"Are you?"

"I can explain."

"You can?"

I used my free hand to lean against my patio table. "I got cold feet."

"Cold feet?"

"Yeah … I'm just not ready, you know, for dating."

"Didn't we agree it wasn't going to be a date?"

"I wasn't ready for a friendly dinner either, I guess."

"So, what *did* you do last night, Jimmy?"

Her uncharacteristic reserve made me nervous. She was sounding a little too much like Mom on a morning after I'd stayed out past curfew. "Um, nothing really. Went to the mall, turned in early."

"Uh-huh, and your cellphone?"

I pushed away from the table. "Accidentally turned off."

"Ah. And where, exactly, *did* you turn in early last night, Jimmy?"

"What do you mean?"

"Well, it's a logical question, since I recently learned that while I was here at home reassuring Lorraine and keeping the meatloaf warm, you were at the Seagull Bar kissing Sadie Gordon."

My mouth dropped. "What? Who?"

"Muriel Swanson."

"Muriel? How on earth would she—"

"Her son Michael. You know, the one who likes to be called Manx."

A fuzzy, semi-complete male image surfaced in my brain.

"He was there," Kellie explained.

"Manx," I repeated lamely. My cheeks burned.

"He took a picture. He posted it on *the Facelift*." I could sense her seething through the phone connection.

"Face … I'm kissing her on Facebook?"

"So I hear. Not that I use any of that social media. Honestly, Jimmy, what would our poor mother say?"

Separating the phone from my ear, I took a second to gauge my reaction. It was embarrassing, sure, but also gratifying, in a guilty-pleasure, macho schmuck kind of way.

I put the phone back to my ear. "… and fools' faces always appear in public places. That's what she'd say, Jimmy," my sister went on.

"That was Grandma's saying, not Mom's."

"It still applies."

I sighed. "Okay, you got me. Look, when I saw Sadie last Saturday, I fell for her all over again. There's nothing I can do about it."

"Will you give me a small break? You're just a slave to love, is that it?"

"Essentially, yes. For crying out loud, aren't we all?"

"Not if it means taking up with an anti-Mormon who writes porn."

A text came in from Sadie. "Kellie, can you hold a sec?" I paused the call without waiting for her answer.

Sadie had sent the picture of us kissing along with, *Oops! I'm afraid this is circulating around Facebook.*

I enlarged the image. Arms wrapped around the curve of her waist, I was kissing her full on the mouth. Take that, Wally T. *We look good*, I wrote.

Back to Kellie. "Sis, Sadie is a lovely person."

"You need to talk to Bishop Haas."

My phone beeped an incoming text. A smiley-wink from Sadie. "How sweet," I mumbled, happy that she also seemed to be taking it in stride. Although it was sure to be awkward for both of us, going public this early in the game.

"Who are you talking to?" Kellie called.

"Nobody, and I've nothing to confess to Bishop Haas. If you'd just give Sadie a chance." I veered back toward the house to see Julia standing at the screen door, hands clasped over her mouth, about to burst into laughter. I took that to mean she'd overheard our conversation. "Kellie, I have to go."

"Coming for dinner after church tomorrow?"

"Sure." I pocketed my phone and walked back to the house.

Julia's hands slid from her mouth to her chin. "You stood up Lorraine and Aunt Kellie last night?"

"I'm afraid so. I went to the City to see Sadie Gordon instead."

"So you *are* dating her."

"We've just barely started seeing each other again, honey. It's too soon to say how things will turn out."

She smiled brightly. "I know, Dad, but I'm still really happy for you." Her smile faded. "Mom's sure going to flip out, though."

I stepped inside the door and pulled her into my arms. "Let me worry about your mother."

Julia squeezed me back and then broke free to return to her project. I pulled out my phone and checked the time. Two thirty. Whitney was probably at home. But a confrontation with my ex-wife on the heels of Kellie's cross-examination was a little too much drama for one sitting. Best to pace myself. I turned off my ringer, went to put my mobile away, and then brought it back out and switched it to pulse mode. After all, I didn't want to miss any texts from Sadie. As it happened, we exchanged several during the remainder of the afternoon, prompting Julia to glance up from her electronic components with more of those terrifyingly knowing looks. A few hours later, my nerves somewhat settled, I turned on my ringer, went to my bedroom, and readied myself for Act Two.

"Hello?" I shouted.

Crackling silence sizzled across the phone line, like a hundred twinkle lights had blown their fuses. And even though she was clear across town I could see the expression on my ex-wife's face. Mobile pressed to my ear, I got up off the edge of my bed and walked to the window. The garden looked glorious in the waning sunlight.

"Whitney, are you there?" I checked again to see that the door to my room was closed and that Julia, still at work on her project, was safely on the other side.

"Jim Maxwell, are you saying that you're actually *dating* her?"

"Sure am," I replied cheerfully. "It started last Saturday when I ran into Sadie at a wedding reception. It's not serious yet, and I made that clear to Julia."

"Not serious? Are you aware that the entire stake is talking about you?"

I chuckled. "I know. Can you believe it? *Me.*"

"Why do you sound so happy? There's a phony picture of you two floating around on Facebook."

"It's not a fake."

"Jim, it's an obvious forgery. Your head is photo-shopped onto some guy in an expensive coat who was groping her in a bar last night."

"That's *my* expensive coat. I bought it to look nice for her. And we were *kissing* in the bar last night."

"You bought clothes? You never did that for me."

When I didn't respond, she added, "Julia thought you were going invite me to dinner last night."

I swallowed hard. Time for me to choose my words carefully. Something I was never very good at, especially on short notice. "Julia knows you are the last person I would ask to dinner."

She uttered a strange sound, something between a gasp and a groan. "I see your manners haven't improved."

I exhaled and rested my free hand behind my neck. "What I meant was, Julia understands that you and I aren't going to get back together."

"For our daughter's sake, I wish you wouldn't put so much emphasis on that."

"And I wish you'd quit telling our daughter that we're still married. For crying out loud, we've been divorced for twelve years now."

"I know *that*," she spat. "I only reassure her that we are still a forever family."

I let my hand drop to my side. "She doesn't seem to find that reassuring. Besides, you and I are not a forever anything. Julia doesn't—"

"You've got that right. Especially if you go on groping women in bars. You'll ruin our eternal salvation."

"I don't grope women in—"

A text came in. Sadie. *My dad just saw our Facebook picture.*

"Whitney, will you hold?"

I paused the call. An image of Bishop Gordon flashed in my mind. I was still in college when we met. He didn't seem to like me much. I texted Sadie, *How'd he take it?*

Back to my ex-wife. "Whitney, stop talking to Julia about this forever stuff. It just confuses her."

"I hardly need parenting tips from somebody whose daughter can see him on the Internet fondling—"

Another text. I lowered the phone from my ear. Sadie again. *Badly,* she wrote.

Heaving a sigh, I returned to my ex. She was carrying on about what she now referred to as my "public foreplay."

"What-*ever*," I groaned, cutting her off. "Can you at least keep your opinions about our marriage between you and me, and not involve Julia?"

"Can you stop fondling women online?"

"I wasn't—" I caught myself, realizing the futility of my argument. "Deal."

"Fine."

We hung up on each other.

I texted Sadie back, *Skype tonight?*

Love to, she replied.

I smiled, slipped my phone in my pocket, and left to find Julia.

With the dinner dishes done and the science project completed, I nudged Julia into finding a scripture on the app. She went along with me, reading through the verses quickly without any apparent interest toward mastering them. Since the passage happened to be that one on repentance from Acts, I didn't pursue the subject. Instead I let her go to her room for an online giggling session with her friend Marnie while

I went to do the same with Sadie.

Sitting cross-legged atop my bed, I opened my laptop and dialed. She answered from her kitchen table, napkin in hand.

"Hi there, Maxwell."

"You eating dinner?"

"Uh-huh. Just got back from Godzilla's."

"Where?"

She held up a dark rimmed cylinder. "Sushi."

I made a face.

"Wish you were here." She bit into the roll and paused to savor her food. It was a habit she'd had since college, one that never failed to turn me on.

"I do, too," I half sighed.

"On the other hand, since you're not here, I don't have to share."

I made another face. "Trust me, if I were there, you would still not have to share."

"Aha, I should have known. You're not a sushi fan." She shot me a dimpled smile. "Meat and potatoes, right?"

"I eat fish, only cooked."

She savored the last bit of sushi. I salivated.

"Would you at least try a vegetable roll?" she asked.

"Maybe. What did your father say about our Facebook debut?"

"The usual tirade about how ashamed he is of me. And then another about how he'd always known you'd end up leaving the church."

"He thinks I'm an ex-Mormon?"

She nodded. "Next thing you know he'll be saying *you* led *me* astray."

"Why would he assume I'm an ex-Mormon?"

"Well, for starters you had your picture snapped at an ex-Mormon party."

"Oh, yeah." Up until now it hadn't occurred to me that anyone might think I was at the Seagull for reasons other than to see her. "I went because you went. Incidentally, why do you go to ex-Mormon parties? You've said yourself that you don't like them."

"Same reason I go to any party. There might be people there who are interested in my book."

"For business, then. That makes sense." It was, after all, the same reason I drank ginger ale at high-end happy hours. But the Seagull was hardly high-end. The dirty version of the BYU Fight Song replayed in my head. "I don't want to insult any of your readers, Sadie, but some of those people are a little over-the-top."

"They are indeed," she agreed, only with a hint of admiration in her voice.

"I talked to this lady whose blouse was only a temple garment."

"That would be Lydia." Sadie wiped her hands on a paper napkin. "She's a sweet person, but damaged, and—yes—a little over-the-top. But then, there are certainly some active Mormons who are over-the-top. My father, for example."

Had to admit, she made a good point. "Or my ex-wife," I conceded, and then added, "I'm afraid my daughter's bishop might be one of those, too."

Her face fell. "Speaking of Julia, does she know about us?"

I grinned back at her grave expression. "Yes, and she couldn't be more pleased."

"How about your sister, Kellie?"

"She's not so pleased."

"Has she seen the picture of us?"

"No. She doesn't do *the Facelift*."

Sadie giggled.

"She knows about it, though. But mostly she was upset that I stood her up for dinner at her house last night."

"Didn't you call to cancel?" She reached for a wineglass and swirled the contents. It was clear and a very pale yellow.

"No, and Kellie had arranged a date for me."

"Really? Who?"

"Her name's Lorraine Grace, she's—"

"I met Lorraine the other night, at the wedding reception." Sadie took a small sip of her wine. "She's quite a catch."

Quite a catch. For a nice enough Mormon guy. "That's what I kept telling myself. Then I saw Wally T on your Facebook wall."

"My hero. So you rushed out the door and drove straight to the Seagull Bar."

"Actually, I made a stop at Nordstrom."

"Really?" Sadie leaned back in her chair and sipped her wine. "What for?"

"Clothes." I motioned up and down at my sweatpants and tee shirt. "I couldn't pick up a classy girl like you dressed like this."

"Maxwell, that's so sweet."

"You said I looked handsome, remember?"

"You think I said that because of the clothes?"

"Had to have been."

"Is that what you had on for your dinner with Lorraine?" she asked, nodding at my current apparel.

"Well, no. I had something slightly nicer picked out."

"Show me."

I rolled my eyes. "A polo shirt and khakis."

"I want to see. Don't you have them there?"

"Yes." They were still in the bag from Nordstrom. I got up from the bed and went to find it sitting on my closet floor.

"Maxwell, that's so hot," Sadie exclaimed when I held up the yellow shirt in front of the camera. "Will you model it for me?"

"I'm sure I will," I replied, laughing.

"I mean now."

"*No.*"

"Why not?"

"You're excited enough as it is."

The sound of a cupboard door closing told me that Julia was in the kitchen.

"Sorry, Sadie, gotta go say goodnight to my daughter."

"No problem. Dinner at my place after church tomorrow,

Maxwell?"

"Um ..." I wavered. Heaven knows I wanted to. "I promised Kellie I'd go to her house."

"Aha, has she arranged another date with Lorraine?"

I wavered again. For crying out loud, I sure as heck hoped not.

Sadie smiled. "Either way you should show up this time."

"Can I wrangle another invitation sometime soon?"

"Name the day. I'll be working at home all week."

"Monday, then?"

"Perfect."

I shut my laptop, set it on my dresser, and went to the kitchen to hug Julia good night. She almost fell asleep mid-embrace, prompting me to fill the glass of ice water she was after and carry it to her nightstand. Then I fumbled through my own nighttime routine before I too collapsed. It wasn't until I was brushing my teeth that I remembered the voicemail from Marcia. I picked up my phone and played it back. *Jim, please call me when you get the chance.* It had come in at eight thirty this morning, around the time I was waking up on Sadie's couch. Now it was past eleven at night. I shook my head. As much as I wanted to talk to her, it would have to wait until morning. I shot her a quick apologetic email, hooked my phone up to my charger, and dropped into bed, exhausted. As my eyes slid shut, my mom's favorite scripture from the Book of Mormon drifted into my brain. *Man is that he might have joy.*

Later I dreamt that Mom was twirling on Ocean Beach, dressed in one of those big skirts I used to hide behind, its hem fluttering above the sand. "Follow your joy, Jimmy," she sang over and over again.

The Unabridged Journal of Julia Camilla Maxwell
Saturday, October 19
9:15 p.m.

My dad is dating Sadie Gordon! **<u>SADIE GORDON!!!</u>** Of course I'm happy for him. After all these years he has a chance for romance. Maybe even true love. But it's also too weird. I mean, Dad? He fast forwards through G-rated kissing scenes, refuses to sing along with love songs, and gives out bathroom scales as wedding gifts!

But the proof is out there. On the Internet. My dad snogging Sadie Gordon. Caught by the Mormon paparazzi. Even kids my age are getting into it. Tonight on Skype Marnie was giggling so hard she could barely breathe. Asked me if I thought Dad was slipping Sadie the tongue. I got so grossed out I had to hang up.

The whole thing is wearing me out. I'm ready to crash before bedtime, even though it's Saturday night. I'll need my rest. The kids will be a handful at church tomorrow. But after church, back home with my mother, that's when my life really explodes.

10

When I awoke, Mom was still dancing around in my head, rejoicing. I knew that Sadie and I had her approval—whatever Kellie said. It felt good to have an ally. Even if she was all the way up in the Spirit World.

I dressed for church and went to the kitchen. My theory was that the sounds of breakfast cooking might assist in the disruption of my teenager's biological sleep pattern. A first and then a second knock on her door elicited no response. After a third, more aggressive rapping, Julia finally groaned in protest. It wasn't until I introduced the possibility of French toast that I heard the sound of her feet stumbling around the room.

An hour later we were driving across town to Almaden Valley. Ordinarily this would have been an ideal time to master another seminary scripture. Only today the breaking news about my love life seemed to take precedent. "Did you and Marnie talk about me and Sadie last night?"

Her mouth twitched but her eyes stayed focused on the road. "You're definitely trending right now, Dad."

"Anyone asks about us in church this morning, you tell them it was just one date, okay?"

"Got it."

"Because that's all it was."

"Sure, Dad."

"I mean it. And if anyone teases you—"

"Dad, don't worry."

I pulled into the church lot to see Whitney walking toward the entrance. We locked eyes. She was as pretty as she was the day we met, and dressed in blue, her best color. But seeing her now, I felt only sadness. Imagine her thinking I might have asked her to dinner.

I caught a sideways hug from Julia before she leapt out the door. Then I put the car in gear and crawled back through the parking lot, receiving what seemed like smirks and judgmental looks from the Mormons passing beside and in front of me, acquaintances I hardly knew.

Perhaps I was only imagining it. I hated the thought of becoming one of those clichéd whiners who took offense at church. Still, if this was the vibe I was picking up in Almaden Valley, what might I expect in my own ward in Willow Glen? For a few seconds I considered playing hooky. To avoid being offended. How cliché was that? By the time I was on the street again, I was heading across town to church, just like every other Sunday.

The two-hour gap between the start of Julia's meeting schedule and mine gave me plenty of time to spare. Usually I arrived early and, lacking the social skills to chat people up in the foyer, spent the time either reading scriptures or attending to my duties as the High Priests Group secretary, a calling that amounted to ensuring that whoever was teaching that week was equipped with a lesson manual. However, given my unique situation this Sunday, I wondered if early arrival was such a good idea. Over the years, part of my successful strategy for not taking offense at church had been to avoid unnecessary situations where such offense is likely to occur. I decided to bide my extra time in a nearby park instead.

The pleasant fall weather had already lured a good number of parents, kids, and dogs, all decked out for the playground, picnics, and lively games of fetch. A gathering of carefree citizens that my sister would refer to as "gentiles." My thoughts turned to Sadie. What might she be doing right now? Walking on the beach maybe? Or sleeping in? For several delicious seconds I envisioned her curled up in bed, asleep in my arms. Then I pulled out my phone and sent her a text. *What are u doing?* A few moments elapsed and she replied, *Scrubbing my sink. U?* I smiled, not exactly the romantic image I had hoped to entertain. I texted back, *Heading to church.* My smile turned to a smirk. She probably thought the same about me right now.

Strolling through the park in my suit, I looked decidedly out of place. Even so, I sensed I was less conspicuous here than I would be at my ward meetinghouse. How was I going to answer the inevitable questions? I weighed some explanations in my mind. "We've only had one date." "It was just a kiss."

I settled down on a bench. In front of me, some boys in the older kids' playground were speeding along an overhead zip line. One of them wore dress pants and a long sleeved shirt with a button down collar. I wondered if he'd skipped out of Mass or Sunday School. None of my business, of course. Then it occurred to me, last night's date with Sadie was none of my ward's business either.

Hopping to my feet, I strode toward the parking lot, determined to keep my personal life personal. In my case, that shouldn't present much of a challenge. The upside to having poor social skills was that people didn't expect much in the way of conversation. It wouldn't be long before the usual busybodies backed off and left me alone. But when I got to the car, I hesitated. After church there was dinner at Kellie's. My sister who never let up. Resting my arm against the roof of my Prius, I shut my eyes and silently prayed she hadn't invited Lorraine.

The congregation was halfway through the sacrament hymn when I finally arrived. I slipped into a seat in the back. The young parents who shared my pew were too preoccupied with their kids to take notice of me. But a dozen or so rows ahead, one of my nephews smiled hello. I smiled back at him. He nudged his mother who turned to me and glared. I smiled at her as well. Then I bowed my head for the blessing on the bread. If anyone looked my way during the administration of the sacrament, I failed to see him or her, as I fell into my best attempt at prayerful contemplation.

The sacrament completed, Bishop Haas came to the podium. During the course of his announcements his eyes seemed to dart to and from my direction, that was, until he came to the subject of the upcoming single adult temple night and fixed me with a hopeful grin.

"I urge all eligible single adults to take advantage of this opportunity to mix with others who are worthy to marry for time and eternity in the Lord's temple."

Any guilt that his suggestion might have stirred was overridden by the unsettling reminder that, thanks to the Lord's temple, I might still be married to Whitney. The image of Sadie and me cuddling in bed resurfaced in my mind. I shut my eyes and savored it.

The first speaker was new to the ward. He was somewhere in his twenties and had just been called to serve as the Elders Quorum secretary. He began his talk with the admission that he was an openly gay man struggling to live a celibate life in order to remain a member in good standing.

I smiled at him in sympathy. Also in gratitude, as I harbored the selfish hope that this poor soul's over-the-pulpit confession might divert attention from my social life. But as he continued with his personal story, I thought of Sadie, who would be sad to learn that this young man was choosing a life without sexual fulfillment. Not to mention Marcia, who would be flat out disgusted.

Shoot! I still hadn't returned the call to Marcia. Mentally kicking myself, I shifted uneasily on the pew, vowing to step outside and return her call during the break between Sunday School and Sacrament Meeting. The second and final speaker was an elderly brother whose talk about his family history was unsettling only in its tedium. I spent it shifting more in my seat as the minutes listed by. When the talk was concluded and the closing prayer offered, I stood, stretched, and was reaching for my phone when I was confronted by Kellie.

"Jim, Bishop Haas wants to talk to you."

I heaved a sigh. "Hi, Kel. How are you on this beautiful Sunday morning?"

"I said the bishop wants to talk to you."

"I'm doing fine, thank you. Had a nice breakfast with Julia this morning."

"Stop changing the subject." She wagged a finger at my face. "The bishop wants to talk to you."

"You mean *you* want *me* to talk to the bishop."

"No. He told me this morning before church—"

Bishop Haas walked up and extended his hand. I shook it.

"Jim, I wonder if we could have a word."

"Now?"

"No time like the present."

"I was sort of looking forward to Sister Hawkins' lesson," I replied honestly, deciding not to add that last week I'd slept through most of Sunday School.

"This won't take long." He clamped an arm around my shoulder and led me out of the chapel. I raised my eyebrows at Kellie. She responded with a triumphant smile.

After a couple of niceties, awkward, thanks again to my poor social skills, the bishop shut his office door and settled behind his desk.

I took a seat in the chair opposite. "What's on your mind, Bishop?"

"A little ward business, also some catching up. It's been a while since we sat down together." He cocked his head. "Just how long has it been?"

"Two months ago in August for my temple worthiness interview."

"So, do you plan on attending the single adult temple night?"

"As you know, I rarely attend single adult activities."

He smiled tightly. "Rumor has it you attended an activity in the City Friday night."

"I rarely concern myself with rumors."

"Neither do I, which is why I make it a habit to go straight to the source." The bishop took a pencil from his leather cup and tapped the eraser end on his desk blotter. "Is it true that you went to an ex-Mormon party at a bar on Friday?"

"As a matter of fact, I did, to see an old friend."

"Is that the only reason?"

Since I now understood that my appearance at the Seagull had generated the wrong impression, I conceded it was a fair question. "I can assure you that I've neither started drinking nor have I begun mixing with the ex-Mormons. I was only there to catch up with my friend."

The bishop nodded. "Sadie Gordon. Hadn't you already caught up with her at my daughter's reception last weekend?"

My chair was growing uncomfortable. I leaned back and rested my ankle atop my knee.

"Pleasant woman," he said when I didn't respond. "She had some very kind words for my family when she came through the reception line." A hint of disapproval crossed his face. "Evidently she's a friend of our daughter's new mother-in-law."

I gazed at him, unsmiling. I knew he meant well, but, for crying out loud, I was forty-five years old.

He let go of the pencil and watched it drop onto the desk. "Of course, she's hardly the temple-worthy candidate we would choose to be your future wife."

"We?"

"Well, me and the Lord, of course."

Hmm, I mused inwardly, the bishop, God ... who was missing in this scenario? "You left out Kellie."

Haas made a noise sounding somewhere between a laugh and a cough. "Well, your sister is concerned about you, too. Can you blame her?"

"Yes," I replied. "At the age of forty-five I think I can pick out my own friends."

"Jim, I hope you don't choose to take offense at this. I'm here to help."

"Yes, bishop, I know that," I said with a sigh.

"How far back do you and Sadie go?" While his smile conveyed genuine concern, the impropriety of this inquiry was clearly lost on him.

"We dated in college."

He snorted. "That must have been quite the experience."

I narrowed my eyes. "What exactly do you mean by *that*?"

"Obviously I meant—" He caught himself, drew a breath, and then leaned forward in his chair and gazed at me in earnest. "Anything you need to tell me, Jim?"

"You mean about my college girlfriends?" I replied, making no attempt to hide my sarcasm.

His expression pained, he repeated softly, "About anything, Jim, then or now. I'm here to help."

I paused to consider this. Because I had been seen with a woman who hadn't been vetted by God, the bishop, and my sister, I was now obliged to own up to every misstep in my miserable adult life. I was tempted to offer my full confession, in minute detail, and going back to junior high. Smiling, I abandoned the notion.

"You're laughing?"

I stroked my chin. "Yes, actually."

"About what? Tell me."

"Maybe another time. Bishop, you said you had ward business to discuss with me."

He cleared his throat. "Jim, I'd like to call you to serve as the co-teacher of the Temple Preparation class."

I grimaced.

"Don't worry. I'm keeping you on as High Priests Group secretary. Temple Preparation is a Sunday School class, so there's no schedule conflict."

My tortured facial expression continued to convey my response.

"Do you know the current teacher, Brother Jensen?" the bishop asked.

Bright blue eyes and a chipmunk grin flashed in my brain. "College kid?"

"Grad student, Jim. Newly married with a baby on the way."

"Uh-huh. And isn't the class mostly young couples preparing for their temple weddings?"

"It is now. But you can expect to have some aspiring missionaries and converts to teach in the future."

"Even then, it can't be a very big group."

"There are four students enrolled at present."

"And this Jensen kid can't handle them?"

"Of course he can *handle* them. But imagine how an older, wiser church member might contribute more depth to the lessons. Especially one who faithfully keeps his temple covenants, even as a single man."

Even as a single man. Even as a loser, he meant. Because only a loser would spend his Sundays testifying to a handful of youngsters about how he rejoiced in his lonely, celibate, temple-worthy life. I stared at the barren, beige wall behind the bishop's desk. It was hard to remember a time when I had felt more humiliated. In bed with Whitney, perhaps?

"Jim, will you accept the call?"

"Bishop, I'd like to give it some thought first," I replied, but only in deference to the man who happened to be my ward leader.

Haas sighed. "I'm worried about you, Jim."

"Are you?" I said absently, still mulling over my predicament. I wondered idly what additional calling the bishop might have in mind for the gay Elders Quorum secretary.

"Yes, I *am*," he repeated, in a voice forceful enough to regain my attention. "For years you have refused to attend the single adult activities. Then, this weekend a compromising picture of you turned up on the Internet. Now you say you have to think about whether or not you'll serve in the ward Sunday School. Since when have you ever had to think about accepting a calling from the Lord?"

I checked my watch. Twenty minutes before the beginning of High Priests Group. Just enough time to catch the end of Sister Hawkins' lesson and then make a brief call to Marcia. "Okay, Bishop Haas, have it your way. I don't accept."

"What?"

"I'm confident that Brother Jensen can handle the Temple Preparation class without me. And, while I appreciate your concern, I'm confident that I can manage my personal life without you."

"Jim, you can't be serious."

I stood up and quit the room without any of the usual niceties. Then, on the way down the hall to Sunday School, Kellie blocked my path.

I rolled my eyes. "Kellie, can this wait until after class?"

"It will just take a minute."

Because I still harbored some well-deserved guilt over standing her and Lorraine up on Friday, I complied. She motioned me into an empty classroom lined with child-sized folding chairs. A poster showing a reverent boy sitting in church with arms folded was tacked to the cork strip along the top of the chalkboard.

Kellie shut the door behind us. "What did the bishop say?"

"Nothing."

"Nothing? You were in there a long time."

I rolled my eyes again. "He wanted me to co-teach the Temple Preparation class."

"Super. When do you start?"

"I told him I wouldn't do it."

"You didn't accept his calling?" she gasped. "Jimmy, I'm worried about you."

"So I hear."

"A week ago you were in love with Lorraine Grace."

"Don't be ridiculous. All I did was admire her from across the room."

She moved away from me, stunned. "Now you're kissing anti-Mormons in bars."

"Sadie is not an anti-Mormon."

"You rejected a calling from the Lord."

I turned my back on the reverent kid. "It was a stupid calling."

Kellie covered her mouth with her hand.

"And speaking of Lorraine Grace." I took a step toward her. "Don't even think about setting us up again."

She took her hand away from her mouth and glowered at me like I'd just lit up a cigar.

"Did you invite her to your house for Sunday dinner today?" I asked.

"I most certainly did not," she replied, seething. "For one thing, her church is in the afternoon. But more importantly, she can't stand the sight of you, not since you stood her up on Friday and then showed up online kissing another woman."

I exhaled and leaned against the chalkboard. "I guess I should apologize."

"Really? You think?" Kellie threw the classroom door open, stomped into the hallway, and then swung around and glared at me. "Don't worry about me setting you up with any more women, Jimmy. I'm beginning to be embarrassed to be seen with you."

I pushed away from the chalkboard to watch Kellie storm away. Then I pulled out my phone and logged onto Facebook. Mom used to say that any apology, no matter how lame, was better than no apology. I searched for Lorraine, only to find that she'd blocked me. I let loose another exhale, this time along with a whistle. Couldn't say I blamed her. I vowed to send a handwritten note, one she would hopefully take the time to read. Then I walked down the hall to Sister Hawkins' Sunday School class. When I got to the door, it opened and the people filed out. Seemed I was too late for even the closing prayer. Frustrated, I headed outside to call Marcia.

Brother Reynolds, the High Priests Group leader, caught me just as I reached the backdoor. "Say, Jim, have you seen Brother Oglethorpe?"

"Oglethorpe? No, why?"

"It's his day to teach and he forgot to bring his manual."

Shoot. My one responsibility and I'd shirked it. "There's one in my car. I'll get it to him right away."

Reynolds patted my back. "Thanks, Jim."

I was pulling the manual out from under the clutter on my backseat when I heard my name. I turned to see Oglethorpe huffing and puffing toward me. As the two lone single men in the High Priests Group, one might expect that Oglethorpe and I would be thick as thieves. Truth was, we barely knew one another.

"Brother Oglethorpe, sorry I didn't get this to you sooner." I offered him the manual. He didn't seem to notice.

"Brother Maxwell, I hear you had quite the time this weekend."

I smiled wearily. "Did you now?"

He chuckled. "You old dog."

Old dog? Did people really say that anymore?

"I've never been tempted to go to any of those ex-Mormon parties," he went on. "But then it didn't occur to me that I might pick up a woman at one. That was brilliant thinking on your part." He punched my arm. "I imagine the ladies at those events are, shall we say, friendlier than those at church?"

A surreal confusion settled upon me. In the past all Oglethorpe and I ever talked about was the relative size of our CPU's. "Actually I didn't go there ... I don't go anywhere to pick up women. Sadie Gordon and I happen to be old friends."

"You know about her book?"

I offered him the manual again, this time holding it up to his face. He took it and stuffed it under his armpit.

"I've actually read her book, Brother Oglethorpe. It's good."

His eyes widened. "I think it's fantastic."

"You've read it?"

"Twice. Say, is it true that Sadie identifies most with that Relief Society teacher character of hers? You know, the one who never wears underwear to church?"

I stared back at him, stone-faced. "Oglethorpe, I need to make a phone call." I pointed at his manual. "And you need to teach a lesson."

"Oh, right." He made a quick wave and started toward the building. "See you after church," he called over his shoulder.

"Not if I see you first," I muttered.

I had just dialed Marcia's number when I heard the backdoor of the meetinghouse open and close. Swinging around angrily, I expected yet another interruption. Instead, I saw the new Elders Quorum secretary rush across the parking lot. I turned away so he wouldn't think I was watching him.

"Hi, Jim." Marcia's welcome voice rang in my ear.

"Marcia, I'm sorry I didn't get back to you sooner."

"No problem. I know you had Julia this weekend."

"Well, there was that, but also ..." I hung my head and grinned. "I don't know if you saw my Facebook wall yesterday, but—"

"No, I haven't been on Facebook for a while. Say, aren't you still at church?"

The sound of a car engine drew my attention. The Elders Quorum secretary was behind the wheel of a bright red Mini Cooper. "Yes, but I'm taking a little break."

"Okay, I'll make it quick."

"You don't need to."

"Jim, there's no easy way to ask this."

"Go ahead, then."

"The adoption isn't going to work. Long story. So Cathy and I have decided to get pregnant. We need a donor, and you're our first choice."

Stunned, I sorted my mind for what I thought was my most convincing objection. "You want your kid to have my love handles?"

"We want our kid to have your heart."

My breath caught in my throat, and then I heard myself saying, "Sure."

"Jim, you're an angel. Go back to church. I'll email the address of the sperm bank later."

I signed off and stared at the phone. The Mini Cooper whizzed past me and then turned onto the street. I decided to follow its lead.

Out on the expressway, I undid my tie and tossed it on the back seat. Then I unbuttoned my top collar button, exhaled, and used the hands-free to dial Kellie's landline. I waited through Craig's cheerful recorded message for the beep. "Kel, I'm not going to make it for dinner this afternoon. I'm ... sorry. I'll call later. Bye."

I needed some distance. As did Kellie, presumably, given she'd just told me she was embarrassed to be seen with me. Truth was, I was put out with her, too. She was condemning Sadie before even meeting her. Writing off her book as porn without even reading it. Same with Bishop Haas. I thought back to the conversation in his office just now.

"She's hardly the temple-worthy candidate we would choose to be your future wife."

Why was this nice guy who was supposed to be inspired on my behalf so clueless of my situation? Why couldn't my own sister just be happy for me? At least Julia was on my team. Also Mom—albeit in my dreams. Even Oglethorpe, while indelicate in manner, at least shared my lonely guy perspective. Then there was my best friend, Marcia, who would surely support me. I shuddered. Had I really agreed to be a sperm donor? I shoved the thought to the back of my mind. All that mattered was Sadie. Kellie was right about one thing. At my age, I was in no position to play hard to get. A moment of clarity settled upon me. I wanted Sadie more than anything I had ever wanted in my entire life. And now, thanks to God, my mother, and some crazy quirk of fate, I had been given a second chance. Nothing and nobody was going to get in my way.

Fueled by feral determination, I sped toward San Francisco, the white noise from the road my only distraction. Kellie liked to say that she knew the church was true with "every fiber of her being." I never understood what she meant, until now. I knew with every fiber of my being that Sadie and I were meant to be together. Eyes forward, I drove on in solitary purpose, with barely a glance in the rearview mirror.

It wasn't until I was at her front stoop that I hesitated. I hadn't even called to say I was coming. What if she wasn't happy to see me? Even worse, what if somebody else was there? The image of Wally T in his lawn chair flashed in my brain. I swallowed hard and rang the bell. Footsteps, the jangle of a chain lock, and then the door opened wide. Sadie wore pajama bottoms and a BYU sweatshirt. Her face bore no trace of makeup and her hair was still damp from the shower. She looked gorgeous.

Her eyes widened. "Jim," she breathed.

"I'm sorry, I should have called."

She backed away and motioned me inside. "Don't be silly, you're always welcome. But I thought you'd be at your sister's house."

Relieved, I waited for her to shut the front door behind us.

"Change of plans."

I took her in my arms and kissed her. She melted against me. Then, as we parted, I realized I hadn't felt an outline of a bra through her sweatshirt.

She tucked her hair behind her ears. "Although if I'd known you were coming I would have dressed and fixed my face."

"You look great."

She led me to her kitchen and pointed me into a chair at her table. "So I take it you haven't eaten."

"No, but I'm fine."

"Something to drink?" she asked.

"Maybe some water."

She set an icy glass in front of me and then rummaged through her refrigerator for the makings of a meal. I was about to protest when she asked, "Scrambled eggs okay?"

My stomach growled. "Great," I admitted, just now noticing how hungry I was.

She cooked. I talked, spilling everything about the day. My encounters with the bishop and then Kellie. Oglethorpe. Marcia. Even the bit about the gay Elders Quorum secretary, over whom, as I'd predicted, she expressed sadness. All this purging was oddly liberating. Because Sadie was no longer an active Mormon, I didn't feel guilty for complaining to her about church. But because she had once been an active Mormon, she completely understood what I'd been through.

"I can see why you cut out early." Sadie set two forks and a skillet filled with eggs and bacon on the table and sat opposite me.

As I was bowing my head for the blessing on the meal, Sadie helped herself to a bite straight from the skillet and then paused to savor her food. I salivated. Then I said a quick prayer in my head and began eating as well. The eggs were surprisingly light and fluffy with just a touch of pepper.

"So you're not close to this Oglethorpe guy?" she asked me.

"Nope." I bit into my first slice of bacon. It was cooked to precisely the right degree of crispness.

"Then who are your friends at church, Maxwell?"

"I'm pretty friendly with the guys in the High Priests Group."

"But no one in particular?"

"Just Kellie and Craig, I guess." I speared another forkful of eggs. "This is delicious, by the way."

"Kellie and Craig are family."

I nodded slowly as the realization dawned on me. I had no Mormon friends. But then, I hardly had any friends. Just Marcia.

Sadie smiled. "I didn't have any friends at church either. Back when I used to go, that is."

I took a paper napkin from the holder on the table and used it to wipe my mouth. "Is that why you quit the church? Because you didn't have friends there?"

She sat back in her chair and stared at me solemnly. "Pretty much. Also I was offended and wanted to sin."

I held up a hand in defense. "Okay, I'm sorry. I should never have trivialized your experience. But really, why did you leave?"

"That *is* actually why I left."

"You wanted to sin?"

"Sure. I wanted to skip church on Sundays, hang with people I liked, and write books about sex. Also choose my own underwear and enjoy my beverage of choice." She got up from her chair and went to the cupboard for a wineglass. "That reminds me, I opened this last night." Sadie took a bottle of white wine from the fridge, pulled out the cork and poured some into the glass. "Would you like something besides water? I've got ginger ale."

"No, thanks." I watched her sip her wine. I was glad she wasn't self-conscious drinking in front of me, and I had to admit, she looked darned sexy with that glass in her hand. Also her reference to underwear just now reminded me of what was—or wasn't— underneath her BYU sweatshirt. "And were you also offended?"

Sadie set down her wine. "You bet I was. By the misogyny, the homophobia, the sexual repression, those horrible one-on-ones with all the invasive questions. Weren't you sort of offended today, Maxwell?"

Bristling at the suggestion, I swallowed slowly before answering, "I just needed to get some air."

"I hear you." She picked up her glass and sipped thoughtfully. "It's funny, most of the ex-Mormons I know have left the church because of what they've studied."

"You mean Book of Mormon geography, revelations about LDS Church history, that sort of thing?"

"Yeah. But for me, it was all about how I felt. It felt wrong that women couldn't have priesthood. It felt wrong that gays had to remain celibate. It felt wrong to be so guilty all the time." She nodded at the skillet. "That's yours if you want it."

"Thanks." I helped myself to the last piece of bacon. "Why did you feel guilty?"

She squinted curiously back at me. "Because they made me feel guilty. Like your bishop tried to make you feel today."

Nodding, I raised my eyebrows in recognition. "I guess I've grown used to those inquiries over the years. Although today's did reach a new low."

"My low point came when I let that 'no premarital sex' rule push me into a wedding." She drained her wineglass. "Such bad advice. I wasn't ready for marriage with anyone, but especially not with my ex. Sex with him, sure. Marriage, no way."

I paused to consider how different things might have been if Whitney and I had tried sex before marriage. Of course, such an option would have been unacceptable to both of us at the time. But Sadie had hit a nerve. It felt wrong that a guy my age couldn't find out beforehand if things were going to work out in the marital bed. Life was too short to endure another disastrous marriage. I wondered now if that was the real reason I avoided the single adult activities. Why take that risk again?

Sadie poured herself more wine and then sat back and swirled it around her glass. "Don't get me wrong. It's not like I'm advocating promiscuity. I just don't think people should get married so they can finally have sex."

"I don't either." I washed down the last of the bacon with some water.

"A lot of Mormon kids do."

"Oh yeah," I replied, chuckling. "I remember those whirlwind BYU courtships."

"Jill Ford and Brad Skousen. They met on Saturday and were engaged on Sunday."

"Married a month later in the Provo temple." I wiped my mouth with my napkin. "Same with Grant Fielding and what was her name?"

"Denise."

"Wonder if they're still married."

Sadie's face saddened. "Probably. Most of them are. We were the lucky ones."

While she had a point, I couldn't say I felt very lucky. Maybe Sadie and I should have rushed to the altar when we'd had the chance. "Do you get mail from Mormon readers who say they married just to have sex?"

"Sure do."

My mind turned back to Whitney and me. We certainly hadn't married for sex, or at least *she* hadn't. Heaven knew what I'd been thinking. Then I remembered that talk with my old bishop. I was single, on the wrong side of thirty, and had a girlfriend who was beautiful and willing. Willing to get married anyway. A burst of anger stirred within me. My old bishop *had* made me feel guilty back then, just as Haas tried to today. Only this time it wasn't going to work. My personal life was my business, and at forty-five I could choose my own friends.

"Do you also hear from Mormons who say they married in haste because of pressure from church leaders?"

"All the time." Sadie took the empty skillet to the sink. Then she came back for her wineglass and bottle. "Sit with me on the sofa?"

I picked up my water and followed her to the living room. We settled down side by side. She snuggled up to me. Her freshly washed hair smelled like mint.

"So, in your experience, how do these leader-arranged marriages fare?" I asked her.

"Badly. The couples only have church in common. In some cases one of the partners is gay." She reached for her glass on the coffee table. "Seems like a lot of the women are frigid, too, like your ex."

My mind turned again to Whitney. "Why are so many of the women frigid?"

"Well, I'm no expert, obviously." Sadie swirled her glass. "But I do have a theory. From the minute she starts to have them, a Mormon girl is taught that her sexual stirrings are evil. Then she's shamed into believing that arousing a boy—even unintentionally—marks her as a slut. If she takes that message to heart she's bound to have a dickens of a time morphing from prude to sexpot on her honeymoon."

"I hadn't thought of that," I replied, regarding Whitney with fresh sympathy. "They make you feel guilty over completely natural feelings."

She gazed back at me, glass in hand. "Only if you let them."

I stroked her on the cheek and was contemplating kissing her when she leaned forward to set her drink on the coffee table. "So, Jim, you told me you've actually watched a Woody Allen film."

"Two, in fact."

"*Manhattan Murder Mystery* and—don't tell me—*Radio Days?*"

"*Annie Hall.*"

"Really?" She grinned. "But you only liked *Manhattan Murder Mystery.*"

"I didn't say that."

"Yes, you did."

"When?"

"At Starbucks. I asked you if you still thought Woody Allen was porn and you answered, 'I liked *Manhattan Murder Mystery.*'"

I exhaled and took a sip of water. "It's not that I disliked the other one."

She squinted back at me.

"I watched the whole thing."

"What about *Vicky Cristina Barcelona*? Would you watch all of that with me?"

"Yes. But then I would do just about anything with you."

"Okay, fair enough." She laughed. "Do you still think drinking a Dr. Pepper is a sin?"

My hand returned to her cheek and then travelled to her hair. It was soft and still damp in places. "Nope."

"But have you ever actually had a Dr. Pepper?"

"I got a taste of the one you threw at me back in college."

Pointing to her glass, she asked, "What about my wine? Is that a sin?"

"Only if you throw it at me."

She giggled and then kissed me on the neck.

"Sadie, are you really attracted to Mormon men?"

"Absolutely."

"Why?"

"Because you're all so clean-cut and cute." She pinched my cheek. "Plus the sexual repression is a big turn-on."

"*Really?* How can that be?"

"It's like forbidden fruit. I'm hungry for a taste."

Fearing the onset of an arousal, I reached for my glass and took a long drink of water.

"But I limit my indulgence to the realm of fantasy." She sipped her wine. "No sin in that either, is there, Maxwell?"

"Nope."

We talked about more things that might not really be sins, also things that offended us, as well as other things I hadn't thought of. Somehow, with Sadie, I was no longer hampered by my lack of social skills. In fact, the conversation flowed so freely that I began to wonder if her wine was affecting me. Also, I found I needed to kiss her whenever she said something amusing. Since everything she said was amusing, I found myself doing so with increasing frequency. Eventually talk gave way to kissing, also to a more thorough exploration of the outside of her sweatshirt. Not a hint of straps or hooks. When our bodies began shifting into a horizontal position on the sofa, she pulled away from me.

"Maxwell, it's late."

"Do you want me to leave?"

The glow from the window reflected in her eyes, creating a shimmering ring around her pupils. "No. I want you to stay and make love to me."

"I think I would like that, too." I blinked. Had I really said that? I swallowed hard. Not only had I said it, I had meant it, and with all of my heart. "In fact, I know I would like that."

She laid a finger against my lips. "But, in the long run, wouldn't you feel better if you went home to your own bed. Patched things up with Kellie in the morning … and maybe even Lorraine?"

My mind told me Sadie was right. I should play it safe, leave now, and return to my obedient, celibate life. I thought back to the picture of Lorraine on the beach with a towel draped across her one-piece. Wasn't that what I really wanted? My guilty conscience told me yes, but the rest of me screamed a resounding no. I'd been there. I'd done that.

This was my big break, my last crack at happiness. If I caved to guilt again, if I settled again, that door to my heart would close for good. It truly was now or never. Again fueled by feral determination, I mentally shifted into forward gear. "Nope. I'm good to go with your first suggestion."

She grinned and wrapped her arms around my neck. I kissed her and then slid my hand inside the back of her BYU sweatshirt. Nothing but skin.

The Unabridged Journal of Julia Camilla Maxwell
Sunday, October 20
10:00 p.m.

Another bizarro Sabbath. The boys were jerks, of course. But the girls were worse. Pretending to be shocked. Acting all self-righteous just because we were in church. See if I get Sadie to sign copies of her book for them! Even Sister Gleener was snickering over my dad and the "porn writer." Like she hasn't read Sadie's book at least a dozen times—probably in bed with Brother Gleener unconscious beside her. At least Marnie stuck up for me. I'll definitely get her a signed copy. Even though she did make that gross remark about Dad slipping Sadie the tongue.

After Young Women, Bishop Franklin pulled me aside in the hall, wanting to know the down low on Dad's love life. Said we could go to his office and speak confidentially. EW!!!! I told him I couldn't because my mother wasn't well. Which was the gosh-honest truth.

Only once I escaped from him, I was jumped by more adults in the ward, all of them hungry for the juicy details. I'm beginning to think my father is the only grown-up in the stake who's getting any.

After that it was home sweet home with my not-well mother, who went mental while hacking a chicken into pieces. I was worried for her safety, not to mention my own. I almost wonder if restraints are in order. Like maybe I should go online and search for some sort of Hannibal Lecter gear just in case.

Aren't the parents supposed to be worrying about the kids? Not the other way around?

I really love my dad and I want him to be happy. But there's only so much of this I can take! At least it's Sunday, meaning all that was on Dad's agenda was church and dinner at Aunt Kellie's—and what kind of trouble could he have gotten into there?

11

I awoke alone, wrapped in Sadie's quilt, the smell of frying bacon my only indication that it might be morning. The sun streaming through the gap in the curtains confirmed it was daytime. But I wasn't oriented enough to know which direction her bedroom window faced, meaning it could, in fact, be afternoon. Propping my head on a pillow, I fingered a yarn tie on Sadie's quilt, wondering if a Mormon relative had sewn it. Kellie had made something very similar for me.

The notion brought on a cringe of guilt. I was lying naked under a quilt sewn by Sadie's Mormon relative ... maybe even her mother. I thought back to the time I'd met Sister Gordon. We were in the lobby of Sadie's dorm. She had large brown eyes and one of those whispery Relief Society voices. Within minutes I could tell that she was totally devoted to her children. Now I had violated her precious daughter. Underneath the quilt she may have lovingly stitched for her. I threw the thing off of me and covered up with the sheet instead, pulling it clear to my chin. Honestly, what had I been thinking? Sin in haste, repent at leisure, that was me these days.

Only, last night hadn't been hasty. We'd made love three times. I rolled onto my back and stared at the ceiling, my guilt making way for astonishment. *We'd made love three times.* A shameful grin spread across my face. *I, Jim Maxwell, had had sex three times in one night.* A giggle bubbled up my throat and escaped my lips. Three more nights like the last and I could rack up more action than I'd gotten over my entire marriage.

Resting my hands behind my neck, I relished the memory. The first attempt had been awkward on my part, while the second had shown promise. Then the third time, just before dawn, had been perfection. In my mind, anyway. Then it hit me. What if it hadn't been good for her?

My astonishment made way for horror.

I replayed events in my brain. The way we'd both awakened

and reached, naturally, for each other. The urgency of her kisses, her quickening breath on my neck, how she'd moaned when my mouth trailed down to her breasts, and then cried out during her climax. Sadie had certainly acted like she'd enjoyed it. But … what if that's all it was—just acting? Women faked it all the time. Or so I'd been told.

I sat up and inhaled the delicious aroma of sizzling smoked fat. Sadie was downstairs making breakfast. Just like I'd done yesterday when I was trying to get Julia going. Could that be Sadie's design now?

I flopped back down on the bed, shut my eyes and let the worst case scenario play out in my mind: She'd had a little too much wine and ended up in bed with her boyfriend from BYU. Why not, for old time's sake? Only he turned out to be such a clueless oaf between the sheets that she'd had to fake it just so he'd finally leave her alone. Now she was making breakfast in the hope that he'd wake up, take the hint, and leave so she could wash off what was left of his presence in the shower.

My eyes opened. Whitney always took a shower right afterward.

"Sadie isn't Whitney," a familiar voice rang in my head. It sounded a lot like Mom.

"Right," I muttered. "Whitney wouldn't have bothered to fake it."

"Sadie doesn't deserve that!" This time it was definitely Mom.

I inhaled a deep breath. My emotions were spinning out of control. First guilt, then vanity, and now paranoia. Sadie wasn't taking a shower. She was making me breakfast, for crying out loud. Okay, so maybe I wasn't the greatest lover. But then, I was also a forty-five-year-old man who hadn't been laid properly until last night. I needed time and practice to get up to speed. Sadie was an expert on uptight, sexually repressed Mormons. Certainly she'd be patient given my predicament. Or so I hoped.

Swinging my legs over the side of the bed, I collected my pants and shirt and headed for the bathroom, wishing I had options other than yesterday's church clothes. Then I went downstairs to find Sadie. She was wrapped in a thick pink bathrobe and measuring pancake mix into a bowl on her kitchen island. When she saw me she smiled shyly.

"Morning, sleepyhead," she said.

I stretched my arms over my head. The sight of freshly cooked bacon draining on a paper towel made my stomach growl. "What time is it?"

"Almost noon." Her smile faded as she took in my attire. "I forgot that you'd come straight from church yesterday."

"Me, too. I wish I hadn't."

I was about to take her in my arms and kiss her when her face paled and she stared into her mixing bowl. Instead I laid my hand on her shoulder. "Something wrong?"

"You wish you hadn't come here?" she asked quietly.

"What? No, of course not."

"Maybe you should have gone home to your own bed."

"Sadie, last night was perfect. For me, anyway."

She turned to me, her eyes brimming. "Really?"

"Yes." Incredulous, I took her hand and pulled her away from the kitchen island. "It was the most amazing night of my life. Why on earth would you think otherwise?"

"Because it's morning now." She blinked, sending a small tear down her cheek. "And you're a Mormon and maybe you're thinking I'm this evil heretic who lured you to bed and had my way with you."

I stared back at her for several seconds. True, last night had been totally out of character for me, but the notion that it was all her fault seemed laughable. "*Had your way with me?* Sadie, in most cultures it's the man who's responsible."

"This can't work if you don't respect me."

I put my arms around her waist. "I *do* respect you, Sadie."

"C'mon, Maxwell." Sadie rested her hands on my shoulders. "You dumped me in college because I drank Dr. Pepper and watched R-rated movies. Now I drink wine and write books that become R-rated movies."

"Sadie, I wish you'd forget everything I said back then. I was an idiot."

"You broke my heart."

I wiped another tear from the corner of her eye. "We should have gotten married."

"Married for sex, you mean?"

"We had more than just sex."

"Yes, but I'm not sure that was a good thing." She smiled weakly. "If we'd married back then we would have ended up killing each other."

"Maybe. But please don't judge me because of my past behavior. I'm not that guy anymore."

"Fair enough, Maxwell." She kissed my nose. "In that spirit, maybe I'll put on a pot of coffee for myself."

"Sure, honey, whatever you want. But Sadie?"

"Yes?" She kissed me again, this time on the edge of my mouth.

"Did you have a good time last night?"

She pulled away slightly and studied my face. "Of course. Couldn't you tell?"

"I thought that maybe you might have been, you know, just trying to make me believe that you liked it."

Her eyes narrowed. "You mean was I faking it?"

"Well ... yeah."

"Maxwell, I'm a writer not an actress."

"I'm sorry, it's just that it's been a such a long time for me."

"For me too, actually," Sadie said, in a tone that implied I might not believe her.

"But at least you can remember good sex. My only experience was with Whitney. I might as well have been making love to a bench press."

She giggled.

"It's going to take practice for me to get up to speed. I hope you're okay with that," I said, trying not to look as forlorn as I felt.

"Hmm." She wrapped her arms around my neck. "I'm totally onboard with the practice idea."

After several deep, wet kisses, we found ourselves abandoning our half-made breakfast for the bedroom where we made love with more fire and intensity than I could have imagined, implying that practice might actually make perfect. Finally sated, we laid side-by-side under the handmade quilt, staring up at the ceiling.

"You really think we would have killed each other if we'd gotten married?" I asked her.

"We almost did just now."

I started to laugh but in my exhausted state it came out like a wheeze.

"Neither of us was ready back then," said Sadie.

"You mean I wasn't ready."

"Me neither. I was miserable as a Mormon but lacked the confidence to buck my family's disapproval and give it up."

That reminded me. "You texted that your father isn't happy about us getting back together."

"He isn't. But now I just take it in stride. Back then I did anything to avoid his criticism, even deny who I was. I was going crazy, so crazy that I went around hurling soft drinks at my boyfriends."

"Sometimes the boyfriends deserved it."

She reached over and ran her fingers across my lips. I kissed her pinkie.

"No, they didn't," she replied softly, and then, her tone turning pragmatic, added, "I was so angry back then. So much so that when I finally left the church I gave up everything remotely Mormon. It was a long time before I could sort through my experiences and separate the good from the bad. Then I was finally able to start writing."

I turned onto my side. "What are the good things that you remember?"

"The hot men, obviously."

"Uh-huh." I nodded. "What else?"

"Oh, the community. On some level I'll always be part of it." She rolled toward me and kissed my nose. "It's funny, no matter how angry I might be at church leaders, my dad, whatever, if somebody outside of Mormonism criticizes my tribe, I morph into a defender of the faith."

"You love the gospel, dislike some of the crazy people. I suppose I'm like that too in a way."

She frowned for a second, as if dissatisfied with my conclusion. Then she yawned and went on to say. "What I love is how the ward feels like a family. I miss that."

"But not enough to go back?" I stroked her cheek.

She caught my hand and kissed it. "No, I'd be miserable. Just like you would be if you left."

"Fair enough."

"But I do love the Mormons' childlike trust of one another," she went on. "Their singular sense of purpose. That's really what my book's about."

"In your book, the ward's singular purpose is sex."

"That's not exactly unrealistic, do you think, Maxwell?"

"I suppose not." I laughed. "Although it's generally beneath the surface, for propriety's sake."

"Screw propriety. I wanted things above the surface; I wanted to explore how my characters would grow once they'd broken out of their claustrophobic shells." She propped her head up with her hand. "The real erotica in my book isn't the sex, it's the honesty. Honesty is pretty exciting to someone who's had to cloister her desires for so long."

I stroked her cheek again. "Sadie, you might be the smartest person I know."

"If that's true you need to get out more." She laughed. "Speaking of claustrophobic shells, what prompted you to lose yours?"

"Who says I have?"

"You're a divorced single dad who won't attend the single adult mix and mingles. Also, you're in bed with me."

"I'm usually pretty obedient." I rolled onto my back and stared up at a square of sunlight on the ceiling. "But every now and then I'm driven in a different direction. Maybe it's a survival instinct, or maybe it's my mom. She raised us in the church, but she was always a free spirit. She followed her heart."

"Sounds like she was pretty darned smart."

"She would have liked you," I said, fingering a yarn tie on the quilt. "Say, did one of your Mormon relatives make this blanket for you?"

"No."

"I only asked because I have one just like it that my sister—"

"I made it myself."

Before long our growling stomachs compelled us downstairs for breakfast, which we devoured. After the dishes, Sadie asked when I needed to go back to San Jose.

"Can I hook my laptop up to your internet?" I asked her.

"You brought your laptop?"

"I always bring my laptop. And if I can sneak off and work for a few hours I don't have to be back until Wednesday when I pick up Julia after school."

Sadie beamed. "Great. Let's go shopping."

"For what?"

"Clothes, silly. You don't want to live in those for the next three days."

We took her car to Union Square for department store splurging. Starting at Macy's, I bought a pair of jeans, some overpriced tee shirts, and new socks. Then came the most difficult purchase, store-bought underwear. Except for my rare excursions to the gym, I hadn't worn any in years. When compared with sex with my girlfriend, department store underpants were a minor infraction. But, strangely, they didn't feel that way. For some reason, any guilt I harbored over sleeping with Sadie had yet to take hold, but going without my temple garments seemed like a big deal.

"We can wash your garments when we get back to my house," Sadie said as I stared at the multipacks of boxers and briefs. When I didn't respond she gently added, "Would you like me to drive you over to the Oakland Temple? I think that's still the closest place—"

"These are fine for the time being," I declared, settling on white Jockey shorts. "But, if you don't mind, I will wash my garments at your house."

"No problem, Maxwell."

Having cleared that hurdle, we wandered into a hip boutique where Sadie talked me into trying on a leather jacket, which I ended up buying solely because she said it made me look hot. I was shaking my head at the total on the charge slip when my mobile pulsed in the inside breast pocket of my new jacket. Kellie. I let her go to voicemail.

Sadie took the scenic route, zooming up and then down both Nob and Telegraph Hills. While I suspected she wanted a rise out of me, I remained nonplussed as we plunged down the forty-five degree drops toward the Bay. After all, I'd been on this thrill ride before. When we arrived on level ground she screeched to a stop.

"Look, a parking spot. Would you like to walk around Fisherman's Wharf?" she asked.

"Sure, why not?"

Sadie shifted into reverse and nimbly slid the car into a slot parallel to the curb. I jumped out and fed the parking meter. Then, stuffing my hands in the pockets of my new leather jacket, I took in one of the state's busiest tourist attractions.

She tucked her hand inside my elbow. "When's the last time you were here, Jim?"

"Dunno. Six or seven years ago, maybe."

We strolled past the long line of people waiting to board the cable car, poked our heads in a souvenir shop, and then surveyed the row of fish stalls. Tourists walked by carrying chowder-filled bread bowls.

"Hasn't changed," I observed.

"Some things never do. Even the bush guy is here." Sadie stopped and pointed.

"The what?" I turned to see.

"Across the street on the sidewalk."

My eyes focused on what was clearly a man wrapped in leaves and branches. When a young woman approached he jumped out at her. She shrieked, and then, upon recognition, started to giggle.

"He does that all day to amuse the tourists," Sadie said.

"Huh. I wonder if that's my old roommate, George."

"Why him?"

We resumed our walk along the Wharf.

"Because George had this book from the BYU Bookstore called *Amazing Dates*. It was filled with ridiculously goofy suggestions like 'do a scavenger hunt at the mall,' or 'have a potato sack race around campus'."

Sadie smiled knowingly. "In other words, cheap dates."

"Cheap and humiliating. I remember once he went to the Smith's Food King, picked up a couple of cartons of ice cream, and took some poor girl to the park for a food fight."

"They threw ice cream at each other?"

We settled onto a bench overlooking the water.

"Came home all sticky afterward," I went on. "Can't say for sure if he ever dressed up as a bush, but it wouldn't surprise me."

"Me neither." Sadie crossed her legs. "I went out with George once."

"What? When?"

"Right after you broke up with me."

"George asked you out?"

"Yes. Wait. He didn't tell you?"

"*No.* If he had I might have clocked him."

"Oh, for pity's sake, I only went out with him to make you jealous."

"I *am* jealous."

"Well, thank heaven it finally paid off."

"What did he make you do on your date?"

"So, he had one of those old Polaroid cameras," Sadie began.

"I'm already nauseated."

She giggled. "He went around campus asking people to take

crazy pictures of us so that if we ended up getting married we'd have this 'first date album' to show our kids."

I literally felt the bile rise in the back of my throat. "Go on."

"There was this bag of props he'd managed to accumulate. Snorkeling masks, mouthpieces and flippers so we could pretend to be on a scuba dive, boxing gloves so we could duke it out in the ring, plastic sword fighting gear, bolero jackets and castanets for our Spanish dance—I had a fake rose between my teeth in that one."

I blinked once, then twice more in succession, endeavoring to erase the mental images. "You endured this humiliation just to make me jealous?"

"I haven't even told you the worst one yet."

"What could possibly be worse?"

"The bathroom stall."

My hand dropped heavily onto my thigh. "He made you go in a men's room?"

"Actually it was my idea."

I stared back at her, incredulous.

"I was being sarcastic. I wanted him to refuse, get all self-righteous like you would have. Hopefully end the date. But when he went along with the gag I was sort of impressed."

Drawing a breath, I took a minute to absorb this information. "Out of curiosity, who took the picture?"

"A janitor. We picked a bathroom that was closed for cleaning."

"Good thinking." I folded my arms across my chest. "And you were impressed with my roommate—with George—because he was a good sport and not a self-righteous old poop like me?"

Sadie started to answer and then shrugged her agreement.

"This is a misconception that must be corrected." I jumped to my feet, grabbed her hand, and pulled her up with me.

"Hold on, Maxwell. This isn't a challenge."

"It most certainly is."

Dragging Sadie along behind me, I scouted around until I

spotted the nearest facility. Two obvious out-of-towners crossed our path. They were both female, somewhere in their sixties, sandy-haired and freckled, and could be taken for sisters. I caught the eye of the one in the Alcatraz tee shirt. She smiled genuinely.

"Excuse me, ma'am." I took out my phone. "Would you mind taking a picture of my girlfriend and me inside of that portable toilet?"

Her smile was replaced by a leer of revulsion. "I most certainly will *not*." She grabbed her sister by the arm and hurried away.

"Wait. Let me explain," I called after them.

When they disappeared into the crowd of tourists I turned to see Sadie doubled over in hysterics. I started laughing with her.

"Oh, my gosh," she wheezed. "They thought you wanted their help with a porn shoot."

"Yup. Now they're in a cab heading for the airport to catch the next flight home to Wichita."

Sadie wiped a tear from her eye. "Their friends warned them not to come to San Francisco."

"Their friends were right." I stuffed my hands into the pockets of my new leather jacket. "Thanks to weirdoes like me."

Laughing all the way back to the car, we drove along the Marina, meandered through the Presidio and Sea Cliff, cruised down to Seal Rock, and then along Ocean Beach past the stretch where Sadie and I had walked on Friday night. Our hunger surfacing again, we stopped at her neighborhood meat market where we took an inordinate amount of time debating over which cut of beef to have for dinner. Gus, the butcher, observed our exchange, gazing to her then me, her then me, like a spectator at a tennis match.

"Maxwell, I haven't used that grill in ages."

"Well, we're going to have to fix that."

"Let's just get a small rib roast, Jim. You can make the salad—"

"No. I'll grill New York strips and you make the salad."

"Jim—"

"Sorry to rush you guys," Gus interrupted. "But I'm about to close up. If you're going to grill—"

"I am," I insisted.

"Then how about my dry-rubbed hanger steak?" said Gus. "Butcher's cut with the best rub in the City."

"You're on," I said.

Sadie rolled her eyes.

While Gus wrapped up the steak, I took a bag of charcoal and some lighter fluid to the counter. "Can you ring these up too, please?"

"Sure thing," he replied.

"Also this, if you don't mind." Sadie handed Gus a bottle of red wine. He smiled and gave her a wink.

Back at her place, Sadie made the salad and then sipped her wine while I demonstrated my prowess at the barbeque. Other than a little rust here and there, the grill was in perfect working order. I had a fire going in no time but then hit a snag when I miscalculated how quickly charcoal could cool in the San Francisco fog. I would have preferred my steak a little more cooked. But Sadie claimed to like rare meat, and the "best rub in the City" made up for any minor flaws. Gus had made a good call.

At dinner we went back and forth over politics, just like in the old days. Only my worldview had shifted from far right to just right-of-center, much to Sadie's delight and also alarm. When I agreed with her about the need for universal healthcare, her mouth fell open so heavily I almost laughed.

"Who are you and what have you done with Jim Maxwell?" she asked me as we were loading the dishwasher.

Later, Sadie beat me at *Scrabble,* insisting she played fair, even after she stretched "chutzpah" across two triple word scores. But before I could accuse her of cheating, she announced, "Loser has to strip."

"Well, that evens the score," I said, laughing, and then immediately obliged, leaving a trail of newly purchased clothing up the stairs and into the bedroom. She chased after me, giggling.

We made love slowly and tenderly this time. That would be the third time since early this morning. Certainly a record for me, maybe even for her, although I didn't want to ask. It occurred to me again that I should feel guilty. Up until a few days ago such a situation would have been unthinkable. I'd been taught that sex outside of marriage was wicked, and that wickedness was never happiness. Only I *was* happy. For the first time in years, I was truly happy. I couldn't deny it, anymore than I could understand it. I only knew that the door Sadie had unlocked in my heart was open now.

"Maxwell, are we in love?" Sadie said. Her head was nestled atop my chest.

I kissed her hair. "'Fraid so, Gordon."

"That's crazy."

"Maybe crazy is good." I ran my hand down her back and let it rest in the valley above her hip.

"No, crazy is crazy. But I love you, Jim."

"I love you, too, Sadie," I murmured before falling asleep.

That night I dreamt Mom was twirling on Ocean Beach again, the sun shining down upon her. "The happier you are there, Jimmy," she sang, "the happier you will be here."

12

On Tuesday morning I awoke alone, again wrapped in the hand-made quilt. But this morning I harbored none of yesterday's insecurities. I was officially a man in love, and with a woman who officially loved me back.

I whistled while making the bed, then showered, dressed, and went to find Sadie. She was downstairs at her kitchen table, clad in her pink bathrobe, and clutching a mug of steaming coffee.

Smiling up at me, she asked, "Oatmeal with brown sugar and raisins sound good?"

I leaned down and kissed her on the neck. "You don't have to cook like this for me every morning, you know."

She rose and went to the cupboard for a saucepan. "I know. But at the moment I'm in the mood. I guess being in love does that to a person."

Coming from behind, I wrapped my arms around her waist and whispered, "I love you, too, Sadie."

As we ate our oatmeal, our discussion turned to the work we'd been neglecting. After breakfast Sadie went straight upstairs to dress. Meanwhile, I set up my laptop on the dining room table and logged on to my personal email. The pleasant patter of water on bathroom tiles lilted above me as I scrolled. The usual advertisements, information about the sperm bank from Marcia, and a message from Kellie about returning her calls. It included a link to the LDS Church statement, *The Family: A Proclamation to the World*. Rolling my eyes, I clicked on Marcia's message and followed the link to the sperm bank's website. It offered the option of making appointments online. I scheduled one for the day after tomorrow.

After that I reviewed feedback from a client, listening to the muffled melody of Sadie's voice on the telephone. Eventually she came downstairs carrying pages from her sequel. She settled into the seat across from me, looking adorable in a turquoise turtleneck and little orange reading glasses.

"I could get used to this," I said.

She grinned and winked at me.

Halfway through the afternoon we broke for a walk on Ocean Beach. While Sadie ran along the surf, I strolled parallel to her on the sand, grappling for a way to approach the next step, introducing her to Julia. I wanted them to meet, and sooner rather than later. But I wasn't keen on Julia knowing how deeply Sadie and I were involved. My pace slowed as the reality of my situation settled upon me. Julia was no dummy. Hiding my nightly whereabouts couldn't be a long-term solution. But I wasn't ready to spring everything on the kid just yet. At some point I would find a way to explain to her that it was okay for committed adults to have sex outside of marriage, but not okay for teenagers. It was going to take time for me to construct this argument, given I only started buying into it myself night before last.

Then there was Sadie. Would she even go along with this subterfuge? The writer who wanted the Mormons to break out of our claustrophobic shells? I looked to see Sadie fish a Frisbee out of the water and fling it toward the drenched golden retriever bounding her way.

Smiling, my eyes followed the progress of a crashing wave as I walked. This was unchartered territory for me. As insane as it sounded, I almost wished we were back at BYU. Then we could have our whirlwind courtship, get married right away, and the problem would be solved. I came to a halt as another reality settled upon me. It didn't sound insane. I wanted to marry Sadie. For the first time in over twelve years, I actually wanted to go to a wedding. And it was even my own.

"Jim!"

I looked up to see her jogging toward me, and wondered, briefly, how she would react if I proposed marriage right now. A jarring image of her screaming and running for her life invaded my thoughts. Truth was I'd missed my chance. Back at BYU Sadie might have said yes. Now I doubted she ever would. Did she even still believe in marriage? Up until now, I hadn't.

"Something wrong?" Her feet and calves were caked with wet sand, almost to the knees of her capri pants.

"Nope. Just admiring the view."

"Take your shoes off and come in, it's amazing."

What she called amazing I took for freezing. I lasted ten minutes, mainly thanks to Sadie's enthusiasm. Then we returned to the seawall where I stuffed my wet, sandy feet back into my dry socks and shoes.

"Dinner's on me tonight," I announced.

"You bought last night's meal. Why not let me get groceries this time?"

"On account of I want to treat you to dinner at a restaurant."

"A *restaurant.*" Sadie stared back at me in exaggerated astonishment.

"It'll be fun, you'll see. They've got these people who bring the food all the way to your table."

"So fancy." She bent down to take a second pass at brushing the sand off her pant legs.

"Know any good places around here?"

We settled on a Mediterranean restaurant on West Portal where the hostess seated us in the corner of the small, brightly decorated interior. I waited for the waiter to deliver Sadie's glass of white wine before introducing the subject.

"Tomorrow's my night with Julia," I began.

She ran her finger around the rim of her wineglass. "So you're heading back down to San Jose."

"I will be, yes. But I was wondering ..." I hesitated, unsure if I should proceed.

"Wondering what?" Sadie picked up her glass and took a long sip.

"Wondering if you'd come along."

She stared back at me, this time in genuine astonishment.

Suddenly terrified, I searched for a way to lighten the mood, make the whole thing sound casual. "Julia wants you to autograph her copy of your book."

Sadie set down her glass and seemed about to speak when our waiter appeared.

"Have you folks had a chance to decide?" he asked.

The menus were still sitting atop our plates where he had left them.

"I'm sorry," I replied. "Can you give us a few more minutes?"

"Absolutely."

As soon as he was gone, I reached for Sadie's hand. When she didn't pull away, my fear subsided. "Look, Sadie, she knows we're dating and would like to meet you. But if you're not ready—"

"Maxwell, I'm dying to meet her. It's just …" Sadie bit her lip.

"Just what?"

Sadie let go of my hand and ran her fingers through her hair. "I want you to promise me you won't tell Julia you've been staying over at my place."

I paused to let the relief bathe over me. "Sure, if you insist."

"And I certainly can't stay over at yours. Not tomorrow night anyway."

"Not even in my guestroom?"

She shook her head no. "There can't be the slightest hint of impropriety."

I laughed out loud. "Aren't you the one who says 'screw propriety'?"

"Only in fiction." She combed her hand through her hair again. "Look, it may be dishonest, but I don't want to be introduced to your daughter as the woman who's committing the sin next to murder with her dad."

My mouth fell open. "For heaven's sake, I've never taught her that premarital sex is next to—"

"Maybe *you* haven't, but I'll bet somebody at church has."

"I know they used to say that when we were kids." I thought

back to a scary lecture from a former Sunday School teacher, one that prompted my mother to keep me out of his class for the rest of the year. Was Julia hearing the same from her teachers?

"Listen, Jim, we can't keep it a secret forever. At some point you're going to have to explain things to her. I'm not sure how you'll pull it off, but you will."

I glanced at the empty table next to us. For a second I saw Julia there, smiling at me.

"But please let her get to know me first," Sadie went on. "I want her to like me."

"She will." I reached across the table and took both of her hands in mine. "I promise."

The waiter returned and we each ordered kabobs. Lamb for me, seafood for her. Then Sadie described the real-life inspiration for the sex-obsessed genealogist in her book.

"She really did the widowers on top of their pedigree charts?" I asked.

Sadie swirled the white wine in her glass. "Actually, the widowers were seated, working on their pedigree charts, and she was under the table."

"No." I set down my water glass.

Sadie giggled. "She was too blue for my book."

"Wait. You told me there's nothing wrong with oral—"

"There *isn't*, Maxwell, but my readers are the most uptight women on the planet."

"No kidding, I married one. For the sake of guys like me, that librarian goes under the pedigree charts in the sequel."

She finished off her drink. "Fair enough. But only in her fantasy life."

I nodded. "For propriety's sake."

"Absolutely."

Our meals arrived along with another pour for Sadie. Perhaps it was the additional wine that inspired her to begin inventing her newest character.

"He could be a divorced dad who works at home and has an aversion to single adult activities."

"Oh, yeah?" I replied, nonplussed. "Based on anyone we know?"

"I'm thinking his latest project might be a game app about overzealous missionaries in nineteenth century London." Sadie slid shrimp and vegetables off of her skewer and onto her rice. "Victorian Mormon erotica."

I swallowed and shook my head. "Keep it simple. Dirty screen savers."

She giggled. "Okay, done. But will you mind if Julia reads about this guy?"

"Nope," I answered honestly. The fictional me had nothing to explain.

13

Wednesday afternoon I was cruising down 280, back to San Jose and back to my old reality. Last night after dinner we'd gone straight from the car to her bedroom. This morning, however, we'd been preoccupied with getting our stories straight for Julia. After considerable back and forth, we decided to drive down separately. I would leave first to pick up Julia after school. Sadie would meet us later for dinner at the restaurant, and then drive directly home, thus avoiding the "slightest hint of impropriety."

My mobile rang. Marcia. I answered via the hands-free. "I sent you an email this morning," I told her after we'd said hello.

"Yes, thanks. You have an appointment tomorrow?"

"First thing in the morning, when the fertility center opens."

"Jim, you're the best. Cathy and I owe you big time, starting with dinner out. Tell us where and when."

"Sure thing. Can I bring my girlfriend?"

"Girlfriend?" she exclaimed, then with less enthusiasm asked, "You mean you actually went to one of those Mormon singles' parties?"

"Nope." My smile widening as I passed into Santa Clara County, I told her about Sadie and described the events of the past few days. Even though we were only connected by a thin ribbon of bandwidth, I could tell that Marcia could barely contain her excitement.

"Jim, you've finally found a sleepover friend."

"Am I wrong not to tell Julia that I've been staying over at Sadie's house these past few days?"

"No. I mean, for now it's fine. But you will need to get around to it soon. Julia may wonder who belongs to that extra toothbrush."

"Yeah, but how do I justify it?"

"Julia is a smart, sensible girl. She'll understand the difference between a grown-up relationship and teenaged sex."

I sighed. "She's been raised Mormon. I have, too. Sex outside of marriage is never okay for us, Marcia."

"Then do right by your sleepover friend. Get married, make an honest woman out of her."

"Propose marriage after a few dates? That's so Mormon. Sadie would never go for it."

"Why not? Wasn't she raised Mormon, too?"

"Yeah, but we're both different people now, Marsh. You know how much I hate weddings."

"Tell me about it. Cathy and I have that lovely bathroom scale you gave us as proof."

I laughed. "Sorry about that."

"Listen, Jim. However you and Sadie decide to be together is fine, so long as you do it openly."

"You're right," I admitted, and then went back to talking about the fertility center. Strange, but it seemed to be the safer subject.

To say that Julia was happy when I suggested dinner with Sadie would be a massive understatement. She was positively thrilled, so much so that she insisted I turn the car around so she could run back into the school and collect her copy of Sadie's book from her locker.

"You don't keep that book at your mom's house?" I asked, as Julia bounced back into the car and refastened her seatbelt.

She made a face. "No way."

"Hmm. I don't recall you've ever brought it to my house either."

"I'm bringing it now."

"Maybe I need to check out that locker of yours. See what else you haven't brought home yet." I pulled into traffic.

"There's nothing, Dad, I swear."

I smiled over at her. "You know Sadie didn't intend it for girls your age. Right, kiddo?"

"Yeah, Dad, I know." She ran her hand over the cover of *Laying on of Hands*. The dog-eared pages suggested multiple readings. "But it's really not that bad."

As I came to a stop at the intersection, I realized that my daughter had probably read quite a few things not intended for girls her age, and the notion was mildly terrifying.

I turned into my driveway to see a flat object waiting for me on my front porch, and, above it, a mailbox so stuffed that the lid no longer stayed closed. Fortunately, since we entered through the kitchen, Julia didn't appear to notice. Nor did she seem aware of the stale air inside. Cursing myself for not coming by the house first to make it look lived in, I hurried to open the windows. Later, with Julia settled into her homework, I slipped out front to empty the mailbox. The thing on my front porch, it turned out, was the manual I'd loaned Oglethorpe at church last Sunday. Stuffing the thick batch of mail underneath my arm, I reached down to pick it up and then stared absently at the cream and brown cover. It could have been sitting here since as early as Sunday afternoon. I figured whoever left it might have rung the doorbell and been suspicious about my absence. But then, since it was probably just Oglethorpe, I told myself not to be concerned.

I had decided on our pizza joint, the one whose business was mostly deliveries. Julia and I arrived to find the place agreeably empty, save for one other party, an elderly couple. The gentleman, I noticed, wore a hearing aid.

"Perfect," I said when we were seated at a table across the room. The waitress appeared, and we ordered a couple of root beers. Then Sadie walked through the door. Before I could say, "She's here," Julia was rushing over to give her a hug, to Sadie's obvious delight. I stood to greet her and she chastely kissed my cheek.

"Something to drink, ma'am?" our waitress asked, once we were seated.

"Whatever they're drinking is fine," she replied. "Same with whatever toppings they want."

"Are you sure?" I pulled a laminated menu from the metal fixture on the table. She waved it off.

"Do you like pepperoni, Sadie?" Julia asked.

"Love it," Sadie replied.

I ordered a large and then nervously launched into small talk. "So, Sadie, how was your drive down here?"

"Good. I managed to beat most of the traffic."

Julia immediately picked up Sadie's book from the chair next to hers. "Will you sign this for me please?"

Sadie pulled a pen from her purse. "Of course."

As I watched this exchange it occurred to me that in order for Sadie to miss the traffic, she would have had to leave the City just after I had. Meaning she'd gotten here early and been killing time on her own before dinner. For propriety's sake.

"Are you writing a sequel?" Julia asked as she returned the signed volume to its place on the chair.

"I am."

"Where does it take place?"

I looked at Julia, wondering where that question had come from. "It's a sequel, kiddo."

"It's set in the same Mormon ward as the first book," Sadie replied. "Why? Do you have a better idea?"

Julia grinned. "Have you ever thought of setting one in the Celestial Kingdom?"

"Mormon heaven?" The dimples popped up on Sadie's cheeks. "No, I'd not thought of that."

I began to see where Julia was headed with this. "Sadie's pretty good at coming up with her own plots."

"On the contrary, I can use all the help I can get."

The server delivered the pizza to our table.

"Doesn't this look delicious?" I picked up Sadie's plate and filled it with the first slice. Then I followed suit with Julia's and finally my own. "The other night Sadie and I barbequed. We picked up some steak that was seasoned with the best rub in the—"

"Sadie," my daughter interrupted, "you know how if a Mormon woman marries in the temple she'll have to share her husband with hundreds of women?"

"Julia, *please*." I hated to see her go down this road again.

"Mmm-hmm." Sadie finished swallowing. "I do know that."

"I have to say this is one of the best pizzas I've had at this place," I broke in. "I hope you both like it."

"Very much. Thank you, Jim," Sadie replied, and then to Julia, "I got married in the temple once."

My pizza slice stalled halfway to my mouth. "You and Ken were married in the temple?"

"Sure. We were both Mormon at the time."

I started to speak and then wavered, taking a bite instead.

Julia's eyes widened. "Does that bother you, Dad?"

"No, it does *not*. Sadie is divorced, just like I'm divorced."

The elderly couple across the room looked our way and the gentleman began to fool with his hearing aid.

"So you're both still married in the temple, then?"

"*Julia*," I snapped, "that's not polite."

Her face fell. "I'm sorry, Sadie."

Sadie gently touched my arm and then, smiling, said, "That's perfectly all right, Julia. Ken and I never bothered with a temple divorce, just a civil one."

"Okay, so how about this. A woman marries in the temple, divorces the guy, but only in a court of law. So when she gets to heaven, he claims her back."

"I'm fairly certain that my ex would know better than to try that with me," Sadie said.

"Look, kiddo, everything will work out in heaven," I reminded her. "That's why it's heaven."

Sadie smiled over at me. "I like that idea."

"Okay, but I'm talking about in her next book, Dad," Julia persisted.

"It's an interesting concept." Sadie sipped her drink and then toyed with her straw. "I haven't had root beer in years. It tastes good for a change."

Grateful for the introduction of a new subject, I swung around to look for the waitress. "Well, let's get you some more."

Sadie patted my knee. "Jim, my glass is still practically full." Then to Julia, "You think a character loosely based on me should find herself trapped in her ex-husband's eternal harem?"

"Yes. Or ..." Julia's eyes brightened. "It could be someone like my dad."

"*Me?*"

"Sure, Dad. Remember how you told me you didn't want a planet?"

Sadie turned to me with raised eyebrows.

I helped myself to another slice. "What I meant was, that most Mormons no longer take that doctrine literally."

"You also said you didn't see a planet in your future."

"I don't. So your idea won't work."

The couple across the room still watched us, even though their plates had been cleared and their check delivered. I now wished the place was packed and filled with enough noise to drown out our conversation.

"I want to hear more," Sadie said.

Realizing I had no hope of diverting this train of thought, I took a long drink of root beer, sat back, and tried to enjoy the ride.

"There's this single guy down on earth. He knows he has to be married in order to earn his own planet, but decides that he won't want one and doesn't bother finding a wife." Julia paused for a second to sip her root beer.

"Sounds good so far," said Sadie.

"But when he gets to heaven he changes his mind, because, after all, what man wouldn't want to be god of his own planet?" Julia extended both her hands, palms upward.

Sadie giggled. I rolled my eyes.

"So now he has to find a bunch of wives," my daughter concluded.

"I see." Sadie nodded.

"I don't," I countered. "Why a bunch? Why not just one wife?"

"He can't populate a whole planet with only one wife," Julia insisted. "He needs hundreds."

"You mean thousands." Sadie took a bite, chewed thoughtfully, and then added, "Julia, that's brilliant. You've taken a classic rom-com formula and placed it in a Mormon setting. Jim Maxwell faces deportation from his planet if he doesn't find one thousand wives by Friday."

Julia put down her pizza slice and burst out laughing. Sadie joined her, and at once my lingering discomfort was eclipsed by the sheer joy of hearing their combined laughter. They were getting along even better than I had hoped.

"Couldn't he downsize?" I ventured. "You know, maybe to a couple of dozen wives on one of those cozy boutique planets?"

Sadie lightly pressed my arm with her hand. "Or an asteroid."

"Or a meteoroid," I conceded.

Sadie leaned toward Julia. "Perhaps my next book *should* be set on your father's planet."

"We just decided that I wasn't getting a whole planet."

"Oh, Sadie," Julia exclaimed. "You should totally write about a sex scandal on Dad's planet."

I turned to my daughter. "I thought children were supposed to be grossed out by suggestions like that."

"Not this time. The idea is too hilarious." She collapsed into giggles again.

"It is a great idea." Sadie sighed. "Only it will be hard keeping it clean enough for some of my audience. I'm always running up against this problem when I write about the Mormons."

I shot her a wry smile. "Indeed you are."

As we finished off the pizza, the subject shifted to Harry Potter and his wizardly pals, characters Julia never tired of discussing. Sadie, of course, knew them intimately as well.

"Sadie," Julia cried, "why don't you come back to Dad's house with us? We could watch *The Deathly Hallows*."

Before I could second the invitation, Sadie was shaking her

head, stubbornly sticking to the protocol, no doubt for propriety's sake. "I'd love to, but I need to get back. Maybe another time?"

"Definitely," said Julia.

"Thanks for dinner, Jim." Sadie looked back at me, her face aglow with satisfaction. For a second I thought there might be moisture gathering in her eyes, but before I could tell for sure, she leaned over, kissed my cheek, hugged Julia, and then started for the door.

"Text when you get home, okay?" I called.

"Will do."

"Dad, she's awesome," Julia gushed, once Sadie had gone.

"You like her?"

"Are you kidding? She's fantastic. Can we visit her in San Francisco?"

"I think that could be arranged." I squeezed my daughter's hand.

Reaching for my wallet to pay the check, I basked in an aura of good feeling. Things hadn't just gone well, they'd gone incredibly well. Perfectly, in fact. I looked over at the table that the elderly couple had occupied earlier. I almost wished they were still there, witnesses to my good fortune. Then, in my mind's eye, I saw Mom sitting in their place, a look of unspeakable joy on her face. In that moment, I was so filled with happiness, so confident in my current situation, so adrift on my tranquil sea of kumbaya, that I hadn't the slightest fear, much less precognition, that all hell was about to break loose.

Afloat on my happy high, I spent the drive home going on to Julia about things the three of us might do in San Francisco. Julia matched my enthusiasm, adding a few of her own suggestions. But when we turned onto my street to see Kellie standing on my front porch, I immediately fell silent.

"It's Aunt Kellie," Julia said. "I didn't know she was coming over."

"Me neither." I got out of the car and waved, while Julia ran across the front lawn to give her aunt a hug.

"Kel, what a nice surprise."

Julia had grown so tall that Kellie could barely peek over her shoulder. My sister sliced a disgusted look my way and then broke free of her hug and smiled up at her niece. "You grow another inch every time I see you," then to me, "Jimmy, how tall is this kid of yours going to grow?"

"Taller than me, anyway."

"Wow, you could wind up a supermodel," said Kellie.

Julia balked. "No."

"Basketball player, then?"

"Too clumsy," Julia said, laughing.

I wrapped my arm around my daughter's shoulder. "The child has her mother's build and my coordination."

Kellie smiled tightly. "Coming back from a father-daughter dinner?"

Julia looked to me to answer.

"We had dinner with Sadie this evening," I said. "She drove down from San Francisco and met us at this pizza joint we like."

My sister's smile faded. "Julia, do you mind if I steal your dad for a few minutes? I need to talk to him."

"Not at all," Julia replied. Then, as the three of us walked inside, she asked, "Okay if I chat online with Marnie, Dad?"

"What about your history?"

"I just have the questions at the end of the chapter."

"Questions first, kiddo. Then you can call Marnie."

Since Julia's homework was still set up on my kitchen table, I thought I'd better take my conversation with Kellie outside. "It's a nice evening, sis. Shall we go out on the patio?"

She nodded and allowed me to show her to my wrought iron table. I tipped one of the chairs and brushed off some dead leaves before offering it to her.

"Okay, Kel. What's the big emergency?"

"Why haven't you returned my calls?"

"Sorry, I meant to."

"Where've you been the past few days?"

"Working, and seeing Sadie. I told you, I've fallen for her all over again."

"Yes, you did." She folded her arms across her chest. "So, the better question is, where have you been the past few *nights*?"

I blinked. "What kind of question is that?"

"The one I keep getting asked. Half the ward's been calling. I've had to stop answering my phone."

"What?"

"You know people can't leave a thing like this alone."

"A thing like *this*? What the heck does that mean?"

"Do you know Francine Oglethorpe Banks over in the East Stake?"

"No. Should I?"

"Her brother is in your High Priests Group."

"Ah, good old Oglethorpe." My mind flashed to the manual he'd left on my porch. "Does Francine look anything like her brother?"

"Not really."

"That must be a relief to her."

"She says you're a bad influence on him."

"It has to be a relief to her husband," I added.

"Jimmy, will you please pay attention?"

"So Sister Oglethorpe Banks says that *your* brother is a bad influence on *her* brother." I leaned back in my seat. "Kellie, this might be a plausible story if we were all back in high school."

"Bishop Haas called, too. He said he dropped by to check on you and found that you weren't at home and that you hadn't collected your mail in a couple of days."

"He dropped by to check on me? Gee, maybe I should have a device implanted so he can track me by GPS."

"He's worried about you, Jimmy."

"Sis, I'm a grown man in good health. I don't need anyone to check on me."

"Not even your sister?" Kellie glared at me, her jaw quivering.

"No." I sighed. "I didn't mean you."

"Jimmy, remember what Mom told us right before she died?"

"She said to stay close and take care of each other."

Kellie's eyes welled with tears. "How can we stay close if you won't even return my calls?"

"I'm sorry. I was going to return—"

"How can I take care of you if I don't even know where you live anymore? Where have you been the past few nights, Jimmy?"

I sat forward in my chair and cleared my throat. "I've been staying with Sadie at her place."

"James Widtsoe Maxwell, what would our mother say?"

Thinking of Mom twirling on Ocean Beach, I was reminded that she sometimes invaded Kellie's dreams, too. "She'd say, 'I'm glad he's finally found her.' I think you know that already."

"I don't know anything of the sort. Our mother taught us that premarital sex is wrong."

"Back when we were teenagers."

"It's wrong at any age. For heaven's sake, Jimmy, have you completely forgotten what we stand for?"

A flock of noisy crows passed overhead. Looking up, I willed my frustration away with them. "It just so happens that I want to marry Sadie eventually. It couldn't be in the temple, of course, but—"

"She's probably still married to Kenneth Smith in the temple."

I blinked again. "How do you know her ex-husband's name?"

"She has a Wikipedia page."

"You looked her up online? You hate the Internet."

"I had to break down and research this woman. After all, she's sleeping with my brother."

"Would you please not put it that way?"

"How should I put it then? And what do I tell your nephews? That you might *eventually* marry her?"

"Just tell them we're friends."

"You mean friends with benefits."

My jaw dropped. That term had just come out of my sister's mouth, and after only one excursion on the Internet.

"I hear that's what they call it," she added.

"Kellie, please stop making what Sadie and I have sound dirty."

"Sex outside of marriage *is* dirty, Jimmy. You used to know that. And the boys will figure out what the two of you *have*." Kellie framed *have* with fingertip quotations. "They're not stupid." She motioned toward my backdoor. "Neither is Julia."

"Listen, Kel, I never expected things to turn out this way, but it happened. It hit me by surprise, like a force of nature."

"We can control our natures, Jimmy."

"Kellie, I'm in love, and with a woman who loves me back. Finally, after all these years, I'm happy. Can't you be happy for me?" I rested a hand on her arm and searched her face for any sign of sympathy. There was none to be found.

"You're not really happy, Jimmy. You just think you are."

"No, Kel. I'm *really* happy."

She scowled her disbelief. "So many marriages have broken up because one of the partners leaves the church. Why would you want to set yourself up to fail?"

"Because I'm in love. Besides, if church was the only reason, maybe those couples shouldn't have broken up. Maybe they should have made more of an effort to see each other's point of view."

"A marriage between two people who don't share the same beliefs is doomed to fail."

"No, n-no—" Stammering, I cut myself off. I realized I was on shaky ground. Who was I to lecture my successfully married sister?

"Think about it, Jimmy. Even if you marry this woman it will only be a civil marriage, not one in the eyes of God."

"If we have love, how can God not be there?" I squeezed her arm.

She shook me off. "I can't have you flaunting her in front of my boys."

Her words thumped me like a sucker punch. I gazed back at

her in disbelief. "What do you mean by that?"

"I–I don't know." A tear slid down her cheek. "She just can't be around them."

"Kellie, whether she's my wife or my girlfriend, if she's not welcome in your home, I no longer am either."

"I realize that," she replied, tightening her arms across her chest.

I continued to stare at her, flabbergasted. "Kellie, I know that you and I don't see eye to eye on some things, but we've always been there for each other. My best friend is a lesbian, and that doesn't seem to bother you."

"Actually, it does bother me, but she's never been a Mormon so it's different."

"Different how?"

"If Sadie was a nonmember I could understand her bad choices because she wouldn't know any better. But she does know better because she was raised a Mormon."

"If Sadie was a nonmember we wouldn't have nearly as much in common."

She looked away from me.

"You supported me during my divorce," I added.

Kellie nodded, sympathy finally creeping across her face. "I knew you were unhappy," she admitted quietly.

"And now I *am* happy, Kel, don't you see—"

"But," she interrupted, her tone turning didactic again, "I expected you to remarry, and in the temple. If this anti-Mormon writer becomes your ... whatever ... and I accept this arrangement, my children will be exposed to her on a regular basis."

"Indeed they will."

"So you're asking me to violate my religious convictions."

"I'm just asking you to keep being my sister." I shut my eyes and used both hands to rub the bridge of my nose. "When Mom told us to stay close she didn't add, 'Unless one of you falls in love with somebody who's left the church.'"

"Dad!"

We looked over to see Julia walking toward us, Bishop Haas in tow. Annoyed, I decided not to reserve my usual deference to the man who happened to be my ward leader. "What are you doing here?" I asked him.

Kellie shot me a disapproving look, wiped her eyes and then stood up from her chair to shake the bishop's hand.

"Hello, Kellie," Haas said with his signature warm smile, one I now found patronizing. He gazed down at me. I stayed in my seat. "Well, I thought we might have a chat," he explained, signature smile intact. "Also, since it's Wednesday, I hoped I'd have a chance to say hello to your charming daughter." He laid a hand on Julia's shoulder. It was almost level with his own. "I rarely get to see her at church."

"Thank you, Bishop Haas. I've been thinking that I'd like to start attending Dad's ward more often," Julia said, in what seemed an obvious effort to offset my bad manners.

"Now I find I'm doubly lucky to see your lovely sister as well," the bishop added.

"I was just leaving," Kellie said.

I came to my feet and looked into her dejected face, feeling filled with emotion but hopeless for words. All I could finally manage was, "I'll call you later."

"Will you really?" she asked, and then before I could respond added, "Julia can show me out."

My eyes followed my only child and my only sibling as they disappeared into my house, the setting sun washing them in a rosy patina. I willed it to go down quickly and give me an excuse to retire for the evening. Then I looked over to see that Bishop Haas had helped himself to Kellie's chair. "So, Bishop, what brings you here on what you already know to be the only weeknight I have to spend with my daughter?"

"I knew I could find you at home." Haas leaned back in his chair. "It's good that we can still count on you to be a responsible father."

By *we* I assumed he still referred to God, Kellie, and himself. "Thank you, I think."

"Jim, I'm worried about you."

"We've been through this already."

"I came by earlier today to check on you."

"Why would you do that?"

"You missed the single adult temple night."

"As you know, I rarely attend single adult activities."

"Then how do you expect to find a temple-worthy wife?"

"Bishop, like I said on Sunday, at the age of forty-five I am capable of picking out my own friends."

"But are they temple-worthy?"

My grip tightening on the arms of my wrought iron chair, I was composing a politic way of booting him off the premises, when my daughter sailed through the backdoor with Brother Oglethorpe huffing and puffing behind. The Mormon penchant for dropping in uninvited had never seemed more annoying.

"Dad, there's a man here to see you."

"What a nice surprise," I said flatly, and then to Julia, "Thanks, kiddo."

She smiled weakly and went back inside. The bishop was about to speak when I interrupted with, "Oglethorpe, what on earth are you doing here?"

"Hi, Brother Maxwell, Bishop Haas." He pulled a chair out from the table. "Mind if I have a seat?"

"Yes," I replied.

"No," the bishop countered. "But only for a minute. Brother Maxwell and I are in the middle of an important discussion."

"And I'm in the middle of my one weeknight with my daughter," I added. "So, in the spirit of efficiency, what are you doing here?"

Oglethorpe took a seat and flashed a grin in my direction. "I was just wondering if you got the manual I—"

"Yup. I did. So, if there's nothing else—"

"I left it on your front porch on Sunday afternoon. But when I drove by this morning it was still there. That's three days that you've been—"

"Neglecting my front porch?" I interjected.

"With a certain writer in San Francisco?" he asked.

The bishop cleared his throat. "I was just telling Brother Maxwell about the single adult temple night. That was quite an inspiring evening, didn't you think, Brother Oglethorpe?"

"Well, yes," he responded politely.

"It was a great turnout last night," Bishop Haas went on. "With the sisters way outnumbering the brethren." Haas winked. "What do you say, Oglethorpe? Take a cotton to any of those temple-worthy gals?"

Brother Oglethorpe's eyes glazed over.

"I thought I saw a little spark between you and Sister Zilpher in the Celestial Room."

Oglethorpe blinked. "Which one was she?"

"Oh—ho!" The bishop brayed a laugh. "Sounds like Brother Oglethorpe can't keep them straight. Maybe you should share the wealth with Brother Maxwell. There's a dance this weekend. The two of you should ride over together."

Oglethorpe and I exchanged a glance. In that instance, despite my annoyance over his presence, I completely felt his pain. My mobile pulsed. A text from Sadie. She was home safe.

"I won't be around this weekend." I stood up. The sun, mercifully, had slipped below my roofline. "Now, if the two of you don't mind, it's about to get dark, and I'd like to spend what's left of my evening with my daughter."

Oglethorpe jumped to his feet. "Can I come, too?"

"I beg your pardon?" I asked.

"This weekend, to San Francisco. Maybe your writer friend has another writer friend?"

I looked away from his pathetic face and kept my mouth shut, if only to keep from laughing. The bishop, meanwhile, stood up and laid a hand on Oglethorpe's shoulder. "Really, Brother Oglethorpe, is that what you want? To skip a church dance for the company of a less than worthy woman?"

"No," Oglethorpe replied, but with an inflection that made it sound more like a question. He stuffed his hands in his pockets. "Well, I'll be going now. Goodbye, Bishop Haas, Brother Maxwell."

"So long." I watched him leave through the back gate to my driveway.

The bishop eyed me sternly. "Maybe you'll rethink your behavior now that you've seen how damaging your influence is on a more impressionable member of the High Priests Group."

"What do you mean impressionable? Brother Oglethorpe is pushing fifty."

"He's very vulnerable right now."

"I am not responsible for the corruption of poor, defenseless little Oglethorpe." I strode across my lawn. "But, as you pointed out earlier, I do have a responsibility to my daughter."

Bishop Haas followed after me. "I'm worried about you, Jim."

"I'm beginning to worry about you, too, Bishop."

I opened the back gate, motioned him out and then trudged toward my house. I did indeed have a responsibility to my daughter. I needed to tell Julia about Sadie and me, and as soon as possible, before she heard it from somebody else. I walked into the kitchen to find her standing at the table, loading schoolbooks into her backpack.

"History all done?"

"All done, Dad."

"I know you want to chat with Marnie. But could I have a second first?" I pulled up a seat.

"Dad, I already looked at a scripture on the app today. Acts, chapter three, verse nineteen. I don't have it all memorized yet, but it starts out, 'Repent ye therefore—'"

"Yes, I know that one," I jumped in. Julia stared back at me, confused. I coughed and then cleared my throat. "I'm sorry, kiddo. What I meant to say is that's a great passage. It's from Peter's sermon to the Israelites. We'll work on it later. First, I need to talk to you about Sadie."

She settled into a chair. "Sure."

"Julia, I wasn't going to tell you. Not right away, anyhow. But it seems people are talking and I want you to hear it from me first." I hesitated, struggling, as usual, to gather my tact.

"What, Dad?"

"The past few nights," I began, and then faltered.

"You've been staying over at Sadie's house?"

My cheeks burned. "Yes. How did—"

Julia reached for my hand. "Dad, it's okay."

"Who told you?"

"Nobody." She grinned. "C'mon, Dad. When we got home your mailbox was full and the house was stuffy. Also, you've been avoiding Aunt Kellie and wearing clothes that aren't from Target." She fingered the sleeve of my overpriced tee shirt.

"Julia, I know your church leaders tell you it's wrong for you to have premarital sex, and they're right—"

"Dad." She squeezed my hand. "I know it's different for adults than it is for kids. You're both in your forties. In a way it would be weird if you didn't stay over."

I blinked. Marcia had been right. Julia did understand, although this discovery of my daughter's sophistication proved somewhat disturbing. I wondered again, briefly, what books besides Sadie's she might have hidden away in her locker. Even worse, what she might know firsthand.

Julia let go of my hand and straightened in her chair. "Mom's sure going to freak out, though."

"I'll deal with your mother."

"What about Bishop Haas?"

I heaved a disgusted sigh. "I don't intend to deal with him."

Julia stared back at me, clearly shocked. "Dad, are you kidding? Couldn't he, like, excommunicate you?"

Her words struck me cold. Would Bishop Haas take things that far? It would ultimately be up to the high council. Shaking the notion off, I smiled and took her hand back. "It won't come to that."

She looked into her lap and in a halting voice asked, "Okay, but you're not going to just keep on … I mean, you *are* going to marry Sadie, right?"

"I want to, but …" My voice trailed off. As usual my daughter was making too much sense. I needed to marry Sadie. Either that or break it off. I was too old-fashioned and too steeped in my religious upbringing to not do right by her. Also I had to be an example to Julia.

"But what, Dad?"

"Well, I don't know if Sadie wants to be married."

"Why wouldn't she? She loves you, doesn't she?"

"Yes. But she's not Mormon anymore."

"She is too Mormon, she's just inactive."

"Her standards are different now," I explained, and then considered briefly that maybe mine were as well.

"Just because she doesn't go to church doesn't mean she doesn't want to be married." Julia paused thoughtfully and then added, "Most of the characters in her book are married."

"Listen, kiddo, I never thought things would work out this way. But we fell in love the minute we saw each other again. It was like riding a rocket."

"It's *okay*, Dad." Her tone was almost motherly.

"And it *is* different when you're older. We've both been married before, we're—"

"*Dad.*" Julia gripped my hand. "You're getting into an area that might gross out the children."

"Oh, right. Sorry, kiddo."

The Unabridged Journal of Julia Camilla Maxwell
Wednesday, October 23
9:05 p.m.

OK, brace yourself. I just learned that Dad is **HAVING AN AFFAIR.** My dad, who wears pill-covered flannel pj's from Target, who makes gross phlegm-rattling sounds in the bathroom every morning, who watches the late-night programming on C-SPAN when he can't sleep. That same guy – my father – is HAVING AN AFFAIR. I'm sorry but ... WTF?!!!

At least I had a little warning. First off, there was the photo of him kissing her on Friday night, dressed in clothes he was still wearing on Saturday morning. Then the next giveaway was tonight, when he and Sadie (who is awesome, btw) were acting all prim at the restaurant. Those two wholesome pecks on the cheek were totally out of character for people who were caught raping each other's face last weekend. I had to wonder if they were playing me. Then I saw the stuffed mailbox and I realized. Dad hasn't been home for a couple of days! O-M-G!!!

So by the time he got around to spilling it, I was prepared. I acted cool, even brought it up for him, pretended I'd known all along. They say it's best not to show shock or disapproval. Otherwise they clam up, won't share secrets with you. It's about trust. Letting them feel like you're on their side.

Anyhow, it seems his whole ward knows, even Aunt Kellie and Bishop Haas. Which means my ward will know by Sunday. Which means it will get back to Mom any day now, maybe already has. I guess I should have ordered that Hannibal Lecter get-up. Hindsight.

I suppose I should be worried. After all, my father is committing the sin next to murder, refuses to confess to his bishop, and is possibly headed toward excommunication. This could put a dent in our family's reputation. Not to mention our eternal salvation.

But here's the thing. If Dad won't talk to his bishop, I see no reason I should talk to mine. (Sweet!) Also, I really like the woman that he's openly fornicating with. Sadie is cool. I can see myself opening up to her someday—maybe even about 4th period. So I kind of don't want Dad to stop having sex with her, just to assume responsibility. Swap out fornication for marriage.

Aside from the gossip (which I can handle) and our eternal judgment (which could be handled with a marriage certificate), there's only one downside: Mom (who no one can handle).

From now on when she brings up Dad, I'll either be conveniently busy or I'll cover my ears and sing, "La-la-la, I can't hear you." Let dad deal with her. After all, he really ought to assume that responsibility too.

14

Our Thursday began before six, thanks to Julia's early morning seminary class. What little sleep I'd gotten had been consumed by Mom strolling along Ocean Beach against the backdrop of a spectacular sunset. "Happiness isn't black and white, Jimmy," she told me. "It's every color in the spectrum."

I dropped Julia at church in Almaden Valley and then headed for Starbucks where I bought an herbal tea and the *New York Times* and then settled into my usual booth. Killing time before my appointment at the fertility center. After my talk with Julia last night, I called Sadie. Our conversation was relatively short, as we were both exhausted. Also, I didn't want to overshadow the glow of our successful dinner with the dismal events that had followed. Kellie, Haas, and Oglethorpe were subjects better discussed in the daytime.

I finished the crossword puzzle in just under thirty minutes, pretty darned good for a Thursday. I made a mental note to mention it to Marcia. Then, realizing that my only friend would probably be more interested in my performance at the sperm bank, I tossed my cup, tucked the paper under my arm, and headed to the car.

Since I had ample time before my appointment, I cruised back streets, singing along to the oldies station, and doing my best to muster the positive energy I needed to produce the high-octane specimen that Marcia and Cathy deserved. It occurred to me that if this experiment succeeded, I was going to have to tell Julia. But, thankfully, I could choose the moment. I doubted the ward busybodies would get wind of this, and if they did they wouldn't believe it.

Pulling to a stop, I waited for an elderly woman to cross the street in front of me. "Even *I* can't believe I'm doing this," I mumbled aloud, and then, pressing on the accelerator, went back to mustering positive energy. As karmic destiny would have it, Herman and the Hermits were next on the hit list. I turned up the volume. Peter Noone had just woken up.

The music cut off to make way for an incoming call. Whitney. So much for feeling fine. I hit "accept" on my dash. "Hullo."

"Is it true you're sleeping with that anti-Mormon porn author?"

"Who is this?"

"Your humor is completely lame."

"Your greeting is completely lame. Whatever happened to, 'Hi, Jim, this is your ex-wife calling'?"

"I don't have time for small talk. I'm worried about my daughter."

"Julia is *our* daughter and she's fine. I just dropped her at seminary. She has a ride with Marnie's mom to school after."

"And what did the two of you do yesterday?"

"Well," I drawled, "I picked her up at school, she did her homework at my house, and then we went out for dinner."

"Where did you have dinner?"

"A local pizza parlor," I explained, and then, gripping the wheel with both hands, added, "We met Sadie there."

The screen on my dash indicated that our connection was still good. But the empty static transmitting from her phone to my car took on an ominous sucking sound, sort of like when the surf retreats before gathering into a tidal wave. I recognized that silence, and, out of habit, foolishly attempted to change the subject. "You know, Whitney, I think Julia may be lagging behind in History. She always leaves that homework for last and—"

"How can you worry about homework when Julia's eternity is being threatened—make that *our* eternity—and all thanks to *you*," she screeched, hitting that high-pitched, ear-splitting note that sent my brain volleying against the insides of my skull.

"Whitney, we don't have an eternity. You and I are divorced and I've started dating someone else. That's all this is."

"You call what you're doing *dating*?"

"My social life is no longer any of your business."

"If Julia's wellbeing is at stake then it is my business."

"True," I conceded. "But Julia's wellbeing isn't at stake, and she's fine with me dating. In fact, she and Sadie seem to have hit it off."

"Julia isn't fine, Jim. Your behavior has caused her a great deal of stress and inner turmoil. She's even stopped writing in her journal."

"How would you know? Do you read her journal?"

"Sometimes, out of concern."

"Maybe that's why she's stopped writing in it."

"Get this clear, Jim Maxwell. My daughter is not going to San Francisco with you to see *that woman*."

"She's *our* daughter, Whitney, and I will take her to San Francisco. Also my girlfriend's name is Sadie."

"Your so-called girlfriend is an anti-Mormon porn writer who's lured you into her trap. Now you want Julia to join you in your little love nest up there in today's version of Sodom and Gomorrah—"

I tuned Whitney out. It was a survival skill I'd acquired early in our marriage. I wasn't entirely surprised by her reaction. To my knowledge, Whitney had only been to San Francisco once. We'd just flown into SFO after our weeklong honeymoon in Hawaii. I thought it might be fun to drive around the City before heading back to San Jose. Only the whole thing backfired when I made a wrong turn and took her past a topless bar, inciting a tirade much like the one I was ignoring right now. It had been worth it, in a way. That bar was the closest I'd gotten the entire week to seeing a woman naked.

"The first Sunday Julia's late to church in Almaden Valley, I'm putting my foot down," Whitney fumed. "I have my custodial rights."

"Wait a minute," I said. "What are you talking about?"

"Jim Maxwell, you haven't listened to a word I've said."

"What's this about your custodial rights?"

"You're always tuning me out."

"Whitney, I'm fully aware of the terms of our custody agreement."

"Then you remember that Julia was to attend church with me in my Almaden Valley ward."

I came to a stop at the intersection just ahead of the clinic. "I did go along with that, Whitney, because I wanted Julia to attend church with her Mormon school friends. But that wasn't part of our *legal* agreement; and, as you like to point out, we were divorced civilly in a court of law. The judge granted me visitation rights on every other weekend. There are no requirements whatsoever regarding her church attendance."

"Are you saying you intend to take her to church in San Francisco?"

"I'm saying that if she agrees, Julia might stay up there for church on occasion—just as she occasionally attends my ward in Willow Glen."

More empty static, only this time it seemed subdued, like stale air leaking from an old balloon. I pulled up in front of the clinic, punched park, and said, "Whitney, I have to go."

"Why? Are you at *her* house now?"

"Her name is Sadie." I sighed. "And, no, not yet, anyway. I have an engagement here in town first."

"Is it with that lesbian you're always meeting for coffee?"

I shook my head and then, just for the heck of it, replied, "Actually, no. It's with a sperm bank. I'm making a donation."

"Jim, your humor isn't just lame, it's disgusting."

"Bye, now."

Climbing from the car, I set my mobile phone to "do not disturb" and then sauntered up the walk to the fertility center. The crack about the sperm bank had been a cheap shot, albeit a gratifying one, and my wicked satisfaction over Whitney's dismay had recharged my positive energy.

I walked into the waiting area to find myself the lone male among a half-dozen women whose ages, while varied, appeared to fall inside the parentheses of childbearing years. A small, opaque window slid open and a young man in a white coat poked his head out. I gave him my name and he invited me to have a seat. Convinced that the females in the room knew exactly what I was about to do, I took a place on the end of a sofa and avoided eye contact. An issue of *People* lay on the coffee table. I reached for it and self-consciously flipped the pages until the nurse called my name.

She was a slim, no-nonsense Asian woman who rattled through the instructions in such a nonplussed, routine manner that I felt as though I could have been conducting a transaction at my local post office. I appreciated that. Then, before I knew it, I was alone in a room with a specimen cup and a stack of explicit magazines. I stared down at the lingerie-clad babe on the cover. It had been a long time since I'd looked at one of these. Thirty years, in fact, when my pal, Heber, and I had run across a secret stash in his grandpa's garage.

As I perused its pages—tentatively at first, and then with growing interest—I was both pleased and chagrined to discover that the pictures had the same effect on me now as they had three decades ago. Minutes later I was washing my hands at the sink, my specimen cup filled and securely capped.

While I rinsed and then rewashed under the steamy water, the reality of what I'd just done settled upon me. It was indecorous to be sure, but what choice did I have? Marcia and I were best friends, and best friends were always there for each other. In our case "being there" meant masturbating into a little cup. Had I gone the traditional route and been best friends with a straight Mormon guy like Oglethorpe, "being there" might have meant finding him a woman. At the moment, one option didn't sound any more indecorous than the other. I yanked a paper towel from the wall receptacle and dried my hands. Bottom line, Marcia and Cathy were going to be terrific parents, thanks, in some small way, to me. Who wouldn't be proud of that?

Stepping out into the sunshine, I turned on my mobile. One voicemail. Kellie. I hit play and held the phone to my ear.

"Hi, Jimmy. Again you're not answering, but since your message kicked in right away I'm guessing that your phone is turned off because you're back at work after all the time you've missed. I only wanted to remind you that I love you and always will. It's just that, depending on your choice of companion, I may need to distance myself for the sake of my children's salvation. You understand. Oh, and this morning at scripture study a couple of sisters let drop that Lorraine really appreciated that letter of apology you sent her. She might be rethinking her feelings about you. Just sayin'. Okay, I know you're hard at work so I'll let you go. Call me when you have time."

I stared at the phone for several seconds, replaying the message in my mind. *She may need to distance herself for the sake of her children's salvation.* Unbelievable. I had half a mind to call her right back and tell her just exactly what I'd been hard at work doing when she'd called. Instead, I stuffed the phone in my pocket, jumped in the car, and headed north.

Once on the freeway, I used the hands-free to call Marcia. Her line went directly to voicemail.

"Hi, Marsh. I'm just coming from my appointment. Mission accomplished. Now it's up to you two."

I hung up and called Sadie.

"On my way," I told her after she'd picked up.

"How'd the appointment go?"

"Successfully," I replied.

"Were you thinking about me at the time?"

"Absolutely."

"I'll bet." Sadie giggled. "Listen, Jim, I'm afraid I need to write this afternoon."

"No problem. I have work, too. All I want is to be near you and away from here."

"Why? What happened?"

I recounted the whole drama, scene by scene. Kellie, the bishop, Oglethorpe, my talk with Julia and, finally, my ex-wife, Whitney, who still wouldn't accept that she was my ex-wife. Sadie listened patiently, interrupting a couple of times, but only for clarity.

"I'm awfully glad that Julia is okay with things," she said when I had finished. "And, annoying as they may be, it's kind of sweet that your sister and bishop are so worried about you."

"I suppose."

"But poor Oglethorpe."

I rolled my eyes. Poor Oglethorpe? This was her takeaway from last night's melodrama? "Don't worry, he'll be fine. If you'd like I can try and set him up with Sister Zilpher."

"We need to get him laid."

"If we get him laid his sister will disown him, just like mine has me."

"Maxwell, you're not really worried about Kellie, are you?"

"Shouldn't I be?"

"Of course not. She just needs to get used to the idea of the two of us, then she'll settle down. So will Bishop Haas. Whitney, not so much, probably."

"You really think Kellie and my bishop will get used to the idea of us?"

"Absolutely."

"How do you know?"

"Maxwell, you seem to forget that I was raised in an LDS home and have Mormon friends and relations of my own."

She had a point. It made me wonder whether her father was getting used to the idea of the two of us. I thought of asking but was too emotionally spent to introduce the subject.

"We still need to find Oglethorpe a girl," Sadie ventured. "I do have one single female writer friend. But she's bisexual and into leather. Think he'd go for that?"

"I don't know," I answered truthfully.

We spent the better part of the afternoon at Sadie's dining room table working on our laptops. Every once in a while I'd pause and look her way, amused to see her swallowed up in her fictional world. Her occasional smiles drew my curiosity, but I stopped myself from breaking her concentration.

Later I cut out to the market in search of ingredients for my mom's Swedish meatballs. I was carrying groceries to the car when my phone rang. Marcia.

"Hi, there," I said. "Did you get my message?"

"Yes, and Jim we can't thank you enough."

"No problem."

"On the contrary, I know it was awkward for you."

"Well …" I chuckled as I delivered the groceries to my back seat. "It's true I'd rather not dwell on the experience. But I was happy to help."

"So how are you doing? Have you gotten around to telling Julia about your sleepover friend?"

"Oh yeah … or rather, the news is out." My voice strained as I climbed into the car. "Julia, Kellie, Whitney, even my bishop's on to me."

"Wow. How'd they take it?"

"Julia was fine with it. Just like you said."

"See."

"The rest not so fine."

"I'm sorry."

"Sadie thinks Kellie and my bishop will come around, but I'm not so sure."

"I would certainly hope so. But, either way, it's not like you need their approval."

I stared out my window for several seconds. Fog had started rolling uphill from the ocean. "I guess not."

"The only people who really need to approve are you and Sadie."

"I suppose you're right," I replied, unconvinced. In spite of how happy I was with Sadie, part of me still wanted the endorsement of my ward leader and my successfully married sister.

"Listen, we'll talk more about this when Cathy and I treat you to dinner. Check with Sadie and get back to me."

"Will do," I promised and then signed off.

I returned to the house to find Sadie closing down her computer for the day. I cooked while she sipped her wine and described her latest scene, thus satisfying my curiosity about the source of her smiles earlier. We ate a quiet dinner, repaired the mess I had made in the kitchen, and then went upstairs to bed, where we made love before falling to sleep. I nestled close to Sadie, more at home than I'd felt since Mom tucked me into bed in the old house on Lambert.

As I drifted off, Mom pulled the covers up to my chin. "You can't please everyone, Jimmy," she said softly. "And trust me, it's better that way."

15

Friday began with Sadie's amazing cheese and mushroom frittata that we ate straight out of the pan. After that we took a trip to Target where, along with some household essentials, we picked up a DVD copy of *Vicky Cristina Barcelona*. We lunched at home on last night's leftovers and, after briefly considering a return to our work, decided to play hooky instead.

Sadie unwrapped our new DVD and slipped it into her living room TV. Snuggled up next to her on the sofa, I made an honest attempt to follow Woody Allen's peculiar plotline. But as the characters' actions became more befuddling, I directed my energy into cuddling. It wasn't until Scarlett Johansson and Penelope Cruz began kissing that the film regained my full attention. I averted my eyes, fearing a reaction similar to the one at the sperm bank. I wasn't used to this stuff, even the milder, R-rated variety. My cheeks burned as I squinted at the television. Then I noticed Sadie parting curtains behind us.

"What are you looking at?" I asked.

"There's a woman out front talking on a mobile phone."

"So?"

"She's leaning against your car like she owns it."

"Anyone I might know?"

"Don't think so. She's blonde, thin, looks like she has an agenda. Sort of like a Fox News anchor."

I froze and my heart seemed to skip a beat. Then I slowly turned and peered outside to see my ex-wife standing smack dab in front of my girlfriend's house. "Whitney," I breathed.

"*Whitney?*" Sadie echoed. "You mean *that's* your ex?"

"In the flesh," I replied.

"She's so ... thin."

While well into her forties, Whitney could easily pass for thirty. Today she wore a fitted turquoise dress with just enough sleeve to cover her temple garment. It was one of those numbers she considered on the edge of modesty—not risqué, certainly, but revealing enough to show off her slim hips, tiny waist, and well-toned biceps. In the old days this outfit would have been code, a signal that she might be ovulating. Whitney dropped her mobile phone into her shiny black handbag and started up the front walk. Meanwhile, Sadie paused the movie, jumped from the couch, combed her hair with her fingers, and then yanked her grey cable-knit sweater as far down the length of her black leggings as it would stretch.

"Let me handle this," I said as I started for the door.

She pushed past me. "This is my house. I'll answer the door."

"Sorry, I didn't mean to take over," I said. "I just thought I'd deal with her so you wouldn't have to."

She turned to me, her face softening. "I know, Jim. But I would like to hear what she has to say."

The bell rang and Sadie waited out several beats before answering. I positioned myself one step behind her, in full view of the door.

"Ms. Gordon, I'm Whitney Maxwell, Jim's wife."

Sadie smiled brightly. "Really? I understood he was divorced."

Whitney coughed and I stifled a snicker.

"Please call me Sadie." They shook hands perfunctorily.

"Thank you, Sadie. Call me Whitney."

My patience already spent, I sidled up next to Sadie. "What are you doing here, Whitney?"

"Won't you come in?" Sadie moved away from the door, nudging me aside in the process.

"Thank you."

She showed Whitney to the living room where the television was frozen on a lusty kiss between Penelope and Scarlett. My ex-wife glared at the screen. Flustered, I fumbled through the sofa cushions for the remote while Sadie nimbly scooped it from the coffee table and clicked off the TV.

"Jim and I were just watching a film." Sadie set the remote

back on the coffee table.

"So I see." Whitney's eyes remained fixed on the dead screen.

"May I offer you anything? A beverage perhaps?" Sadie asked.

Whitney's glare transferred to me. "Thank you, I don't drink."

I rolled my eyes.

"You don't?" Sadie's smile now bordered on menacing. "Not even water? That is Spartan indeed."

A glimmer of uncertainty surfaced on Whitney's face.

"I also have juice, milk, ginger ale, sparkling water," Sadie added.

"I'm not thirsty."

"Then why don't we all sit down?" Sadie motioned Whitney to a chair and me onto the couch next to her. "And Whitney can tell us why she's here."

"Exactly why are you here, Whitney?" I asked.

"Since you told me you intend to bring Julia for visits, I wanted to assess the character of the home she'd be staying in. Also the ward she might attend."

Sadie's smile faded. "Any assessment of my home will have to be conducted from here in the living room. I'm not open for inspections."

Whitney nodded to the DVD cover on the coffee table. "I can see quite a bit from here."

"As for the ward," Sadie went on. "I can't be of much help as I don't attend. But the nearest meetinghouse is only a few blocks away on—"

"Your bishop claims he knows you well."

"Bishop Wu? You talked to him?" Sadie asked.

"Yes. Last night at length and then again just now. He's on his way over."

"Whitney, you had no business inviting the bishop to Sadie's house," I said.

Sadie reached over and squeezed my knee. Whitney stared at the gesture, obviously repulsed.

"Jim is right, of course." Sadie's hand remained firmly on my knee. "But in this case, I don't mind. Bishop Wu is a friend."

"So I hear," Whitney replied, still glowering at the sight of Sadie's hand on my knee. "The bishop said that you and he have had many long conversations. In fact, he admitted there are several men in the ward who've cultivated your friendship. I assume here, in your house?"

"In my living room, yes," Sadie replied evenly.

"Whitney, you know very well that it's routine for ward leaders to drop in on inactive members from time to time," I told her, my voice rising. "Don't insinuate it's more than that."

"I'd hate to think that somebody might spread any false information," Sadie added. "They're all upstanding, married family men."

"As are some of the characters in your book, correct?" Whitney asked.

"Whitney, knock it off," I snapped.

The doorbell rang. All three of us jumped to our feet.

"Stop," Sadie said. "This is my house. I'll answer it." She walked to the door and opened it wide. "Bishop Wu, please come in."

"Thank you." Lean, cheerful, and somewhere in his thirties, Bishop Wu eagerly shook Sadie's hand. "So nice of you to invite me over."

Sadie stared at him for a second, obviously confused, before saying, "This is my friend, Jim Maxwell, and his former wife, Whitney Maxwell."

Now it was the bishop who appeared confused, but he shook our hands politely without comment.

Sensing another of my ex-wife's manipulations, I waited for Sadie to invite us to sit and then, turning to Bishop Wu, said, "Actually, Sadie and I only learned that you were coming over about a minute ago."

The bishop frowned. "Really? Your wife said you and Sadie were expecting me."

"I only meant that I thought they were at home," Whitney explained.

"Thought they were? You mean you didn't know?" Bishop Wu asked.

"Well, when I got here I saw Jim's car," said Whitney.

"You thought they were here because of his car? Did Jim and Sadie even know you were dropping by?"

"No, Bishop." I glared over at Whitney. "We had no idea my ex-wife was dropping by."

"Sadie, I apologize," said the bishop. "I understood that this afternoon's meeting had been arranged yesterday evening and that Sister Maxwell was going to call me when she knew the exact time." Then to me, "By the way, did I hear you refer to Sister Maxwell as your *ex*-wife just now?"

"Yes," I replied, still glaring at Whitney.

Whitney looked back at me defiantly. "We were married in the Oakland Temple, Jim."

I turned to the bishop. He appeared to be puzzled. "Whitney and I were, in fact, married in the Oakland temple, Bishop Wu. But that was a long time ago. We've since divorced and now I'm dating Sadie."

"But only temporally," Whitney added.

I sighed. "Temporally, yes."

"I'm confused," Bishop Wu said. "Exactly what is only temporal?"

Whitney motioned toward Sadie. "Jim's relationship with Ms. Gordon is, of course, only temporary. Whereas, his *wedding* to me took place in the temple."

"I see," said the bishop. "But then you divorced, right?"

"No," Whitney replied.

"Yes, we *did*," I said.

Whitney shook her head. "Not in the temple."

Sadie took my arm and smiled sweetly. "Bishop Wu, I think what Whitney is trying to say is that I only have the mere span of this life to finish having my way with him."

Bishop Wu grinned. "Uh-huh."

"That doesn't leave me much time," Sadie added.

Whitney looked daggers at Sadie. I struggled to speak but the words wouldn't come.

"But that's okay." My girlfriend smiled serenely. "I do my best work when I'm up against a deadline."

The bishop chuckled. "This is beginning to sound like one of your plots."

"It's really not, Bishop Wu," I said. "Whitney and I divorced in a court of law twelve years ago. Sadie and I just recently began dating."

Wu nodded slowly. "So you and Sadie are both single?"

"Of course." I glared at Whitney again.

"Sister Maxwell." The bishop leaned toward her and rested his elbows on his knees. "I don't see how any of this is my concern. Why did you ask me over?"

"I wanted you to see the indecent environment my minor child might be exposed to."

A wisp of a grin appeared on the bishop's face. "If you remember, I agreed to become involved because I was worried that a single woman in my ward might be unknowingly involved with a married man."

Sadie laughed softly and kissed my shoulder. Her hand was still tucked inside my arm.

"Clearly that's not the case." Bishop Wu straightened in his seat. "But, Sadie, I was going to contact you anyway."

"Oh, really?" she replied. "How come?"

"I got a call from your father."

Sadie's grip on me tightened. "What did he want this time?"

"He's concerned about you and asked me if I knew of any problems you might be encountering. Evidently he isn't available to drive in from Manteca because your mother is out of town."

"Right." Sadie nodded vigorously. "And he knows he can't visit without Mom."

Bishop Wu smiled over at me. "I assume by problems he meant Brother Maxwell here. I'll let him know things are fine."

"Also that he can't visit without Mom," Sadie repeated. "He knows that, right?"

"I understood that to be the reason he called me," Wu replied.

"Sadie," I said, "maybe I should pay a visit to your father."

She let go of my arm and stared at me with an intensity I'd not seen in her before. "Not without Mom, Jim."

"Bishop Wu," said Whitney, "how can you assure Sadie's father that things here are fine when his daughter and my husband are clearly living in sin?"

"Ex-husband," I said. "And you have no knowledge of how we're living."

"Sister Maxwell," the bishop replied, "if Sadie and Jim have anything personal that they want to confide, I'm sure they know they can call me. But right now, from where I sit, everything does look fine."

Whitney grabbed the DVD cover from off the coffee table and held it up for him to see. "You call *this* fine?"

Wu pulled a pair of slim reading glasses from his shirt pocket and peered through them to the title. A grin spread across his face. "My wife and I saw this in the theater and loved it." He took off his glasses. "There's that hilarious scene where Penelope Cruz fires the pistol."

A smile relaxed across my face. I liked this guy.

"We haven't gotten that far into the story yet," Sadie told him.

"Oh." The bishop folded his glasses and returned them to his pocket. "Then don't let me spoil it for you."

Whitney crossed her slim legs and let her foot swing swiftly back and forth. Bishop Wu leaned back and studied her for a few seconds, his fingers drumming the arm of his chair.

"Sister Maxwell," he said, "it's none of my business, but wouldn't you rather find a new husband? After all, Jim's moved on with his life. I imagine he'd agree to a temple divorce." The bishop looked to me. "You would, wouldn't you?"

"Lord, yes," I replied.

He turned back to Whitney. "You could remarry in the temple, then."

She shook her head. "I don't mind sharing him here on earth. After all, in the Celestial Kingdom I'll need to share him."

Too frustrated to speak, I covered my face with my hands. An extended silence ensued, punctuated only by Bishop Wu's light tapping on the arm of his chair. Finally Whitney cleared her throat. I looked at her through parted fingers.

"Bishop," she began primly, "I understand that your ward is, shall we say, unusual. That it's a home to gays and lesbians, childless couples, working mothers, singles, and people in otherwise alternative living arrangements. Is that true?"

"That is true." Bishop Wu slapped a hand on each knee and stood. "You folks will fit in fine."

Sadie and I came eagerly to our feet. Whitney rose slowly after us.

"Nice of you to drop by, Bishop Wu," said Sadie.

"Always a pleasure. Thank you for receiving me on such short notice." Then to me, "Our ward meets at eleven on Sunday mornings. I hope you'll join us sometime."

"Thanks, I'll take you up on that."

Bishop Wu nodded his goodbye to Whitney and quickly made his exit. I closed the door behind him and then swung around and glared at my ex-wife. "If you don't mind, Sadie and I would like to finish watching our movie."

She glowered back at me. "I was just leaving."

"Fine. I'll walk you out." I waited for Whitney to step onto the porch before turning to Sadie. "I'll just be a minute."

"No problem," she replied easily. "I'll rewind the movie back to the beginning of that scene we were watching."

Whitney and I strode down the front steps and along the sidewalk, utterly silent and an arm's length apart. When we reached her car I lit into her. "That was quite a stunt you pulled."

"It was no stunt—"

"Don't even think of trying it again." I jabbed a finger at her face. "The next time you show up unannounced you won't get past the front door, nor will anyone else you've tricked into joining you."

She stuck a hand on her hip. "I will do whatever it takes to protect my daughter from indecent—"

"Julia is *our* daughter, Whitney, and there's nothing indecent about my friendship with Sadie. Ask her bishop."

"You mean Bishop Wu who watches porn?"

"Woody Allen is not porn."

"What I saw of that movie certainly was. And Bishop Wu is turning a blind eye to your cohabitation with Sadie. That's *unconscionable.*"

"He's minding his own business. That's *appropriate*, Whitney."

"Appropriate? I suppose you also think it's appropriate that he lets his ward be gay?"

I stared back at her, struggling to suppress a sudden urge to burst out laughing. "As a matter of fact, I do."

Whitney shook her head and some blonde curls fell across her brow. "Jim Maxwell, what has happened to you? You know what our leaders teach about both homosexuality *and* sex outside of marriage." Her blue eyes brightened and she leaned against the hood of her car, causing her dress to hike an inch up her shapely thighs. For a split second a horrifying sensation resurfaced from the old days, back when I thought she was sexiest when she was mad.

Taking my eyes off of her legs, I said, "Whatever you think of him, Bishop Wu is right about a temple divorce. We are not married. You need to accept that, at least for Julia's sake. You're just confusing her."

"*I'm* confusing her? What about you? Running off with that anti-Mormon author you've known for less than a month."

"I haven't run off, and you know that Sadie and I have known each other for far more than a month. We were college sweethearts."

"Yes. You kept a picture of her." Whitney gazed up at the sky. "I see she's put on weight since then." She turned back to me. "I understand that's not unusual for people who leave the church. They ... indulge."

I shut my eyes. "She makes me happy, Whitney. From the minute she walked back into my life—"

"I know why you like her, Jim."

I opened my eyes to see that her face had saddened.

"I just hold out hope that in the next life, I can make you ..." Her voice wavered. "That we can be happy together."

"You can be happy now, Whit. If you'd just get some professional help and—"

"I don't need *help*, Jim."

I stared down at the pavement for a few seconds. It was as impenetrable as the space between us. "Bishop Wu's a good egg, Whitney," I said finally.

"He's a liberal," she replied.

"Julia won't be seeing much of him." I took a step backward. "I still think she should go to church with her Mormon friends from school." Whitney started to speak and I shushed her with another jab of my finger. "And don't even think about barging in on Sadie and me again. You need to see me, then call first."

Convinced our conversation had outlived its usefulness, I turned and retreated toward the house. Whitney kept talking, something about liberals, and porn, and *her* daughter. By the time I reached the porch, her ramblings were unintelligible. When I closed the door behind me they shut off completely. I paused in the entryway, relishing the silence. Then Sadie emerged from the kitchen carrying a glass of white wine.

"Well." I smiled and rubbed my hands together. "That's my ex."

Sadie nodded. "She's charming, Maxwell."

The rest of the afternoon went pleasantly enough. Like Bishop

Wu said, the part where Penelope Cruz fired the pistol was hilarious. But when the film ended and we began to think about dinner, Sadie's mood took a downturn.

"I can't have pasta," she insisted.

"Why the heck not?" I put the box of spaghetti on the kitchen island.

Sadie slapped her hands on her hips. "I'm too fat."

"What?"

"I saw your ex-wife, Jim. Her figure is perfect."

"Honey, please don't compare yourself to her."

"How can I not? She's gorgeous."

"No. You're gorgeous."

She squeezed her thighs. "I'm nothing but blubber. Whitney's all muscle. Does she work out?"

"Constantly." I rolled my eyes. "It's her one turn-on."

Sadie moved her hands back up to her hips. "I can't believe how I've let myself go," she moaned.

"Look at me." I reached down and grabbed my love handles. "It's not like I couldn't stand to lose a few."

Her face took on an expression of crazed defensiveness. "It's different for men."

It's different for men. I knew the phrase well. It was a designation that might ignite any number of gender-specific powder kegs. Rather than wander into a potential minefield, I dropped my end of the argument, went to the refrigerator, and found a head of lettuce for Sadie to make into a salad.

We faded fast that evening, both of us exhausted after the emotional rigors of the day. But I managed to draw a smile when I suggested we go upstairs and "work out together." In spite of our fatigue, we had a lively go at it, and Sadie fell right to sleep afterward. I remained awake, gripped by an unidentifiable anxiousness I couldn't quite put my finger on, the nagging, yet utterly baseless fear that another shoe was about to drop.

The Unabridged Journal of Julia Camilla Maxwell
Thursday, October 24
8:45 p.m.

Mom was over the top bonkers tonight. Going on about how she's taking over my moral upbringing and that I am never to see my father again, or Sadie, or some character she called Bishop Woo. I'm proud to say I tuned her out. It's a newfound skill I'm grateful to have acquired. But that didn't keep me from seeing her hurl the food on the kitchen counter, attack it with her knife and then murder it in the pan. When she finished with it, tonight's pork stir-fry looked more like pureed Spam.

After what passed for dinner I managed to escape to my room, claiming I had bad cramps, my stomach was a war zone, and my head was about to explode. All of that was true except for the cramps. I took three Advil and am now buried under my comforter with my headphones on and barely enough light to see the page. Any ranting outside my door is drowned out by Pandora.

From the time Dad dropped me at seminary yesterday I'd been bracing myself for her reaction, on edge through two entire school days, even during 4th period. I was expecting tears, hand wringing, bemoaning our doomed eternity. (We're not doomed, Mom.) Begging me to tell her everything I know. (Nothing, Mom.) Had I met Sadie? (Once, briefly. It wasn't very interesting.) All the while I'd be searching for some polite way of ending the conversation. (Yeah, well, here's a box of Kleenex. I'm going to my room.)

Instead … kaboom! Mushroom cloud.

She actually went to see them! My mother travelled to "Sodom and Gomorrah" to confront my father and "his harlot." From what little I could decipher from Mom's disjointed rambling, Sadie, who was dressed like a hooker, had been entertaining my father with a porn video.

Given that Mom has used "porn" and "hooker" to describe a

spectrum of scenarios, from the XXX movie theater to a Pine Sol commercial, I'm left to measure this disaster against the Richter scale of her hysteria. She was way more worked up than she was over the Pine Sol ad, so: Parents Strongly Cautioned. On the other hand, had she witnessed my father watching actual porn, she'd be in the hospital now recovering from a cardiac arrest. I'm guessing it was an "R" rated movie and that Sadie's sweater was off the shoulder. Meaning I best lie low and keep my headset on for at least another hour. Thank heaven the Advil is kicking in.

16

We slept in on Saturday and Sadie prepared a late breakfast, French toast for me, half a grapefruit for her. After that we assembled a low-calorie vegetarian stew, and set it to work in the slow cooker. Since Sadie had her writers' critique group at a nearby bookstore café, I decided to get out of the house as well and spent the afternoon holed up with my laptop at the local Starbucks. Sometime around four p.m. my stomach began to growl. I decided to pack up and head to the market. To heck with Sadie's diet. Vegetable soup wasn't going to be enough to satisfy the hunger I'd worked up since breakfast. I picked up a loaf of French bread, some pasta salad, and a quart of chocolate chip ice cream. Then I headed back to Sadie's house.

I pulled up in her drive and retrieved the groceries from the trunk, also the jumbo pack of toilet tissue we'd forgotten to bring in after our trip to Target yesterday. I jogged up the front steps, unlocked the door with the key she'd given me, and inhaled the rich aroma of simmering stew. My stomach growled again. I closed the door behind me and pocketed the key. Then I spotted him.

"Whoa!" The jumbo pack fell out from under my arm and bounced across the wooden floor. I stared at the man sitting on our living room sofa. He looked vaguely familiar.

"Hello, Jim. I'm President Gordon."

"President. What a surprise," I breathed.

I set the grocery bag on the dining room table, stepped over the toilet paper and went to the living room to shake his hand. He rose, briefly locked me in a firm handshake, and then we both sat down. Other than the salt and pepper hair, President Gordon was the same tall, stern, and blandly handsome man I'd briefly met when I was a student at BYU. Only back then he was merely "Bishop Gordon."

My heart pounding, I paused to catch my breath. "Sadie didn't mention that you were coming."

"I didn't tell her."

"Oh, well, I'll give her a call now."

Trying not to appear nervous, I pulled my mobile out of my shirt pocket and fumbled with the passcode, botching it on my first attempt. Then I scrolled to Sadie's name in my contact list and waited anxiously for the call to connect. A knot began to form in my stomach.

"Maxwell," she said after the second ring.

"Hi … um, guess what?" I smiled at the president; he did not reciprocate. "Your dad's here."

"What? *No.*"

I looked into my lap. "Yes."

"By himself?"

"Yes."

"Don't let him in. I'm on my way there now."

I got up and retreated toward the kitchen, picking up the groceries and toilet paper on my way.

"He *is* in," I whispered. "He was on the couch when I got here."

"How'd he get in this time?"

"I assumed with a key."

I set the toilet paper and groceries on the counter, rooted the bag for the ice cream, and shoved it in the freezer. Then I spotted a dirty bowl and spoon by the crockpot and, looking beyond them, dropped my phone onto the floor.

"Jim? Are you there?" Sadie shouted.

I bent down and reached for my mobile. It had slid into the pile of broken glass. "Sadie, you're not going to believe this, but I think your father busted your sliding glass door."

"Shoot! The last time he used a credit card on the window and I had to buy a better lock. Now I need a whole new door?"

I stared at the shattered mess, incredulous. "Well, at least a new pane of glass."

"Jim, I'll be there as fast as I can. Meanwhile, whatever you do, *don't* talk to him."

"How am I supposed to manage that?"

"Tell him you have to work and then go in the spare bedroom and lock the door."

I separated the phone from my ear for a couple of seconds and then replied, "I'm perfectly capable of carrying on a conversation with your father."

"Jim, when my father drops in by himself, he doesn't converse. He interrogates. Don't talk to him."

"Yeah, okay, just drive safely."

I hung up and returned to the living room. President Gordon was still sitting on the sofa, looking smug and nonplussed. My shock shifted to anger.

"Sadie's on her way," I said.

The president nodded perfunctorily. "Sit down, Jim."

I took a seat opposite him. "I see you helped yourself to a bowl of soup."

He shrugged. "I was hungry after the long drive in from the Central Valley."

"And you broke in the back door."

"It was unavoidable. My daughter hasn't given me a key. And she's apparently installed a new lock on her bedroom window."

"You tried to come in her bedroom—"

"As I said, I don't have a key."

"Yes, but why didn't you simply call her—"

"Because I'm her *father*," he announced.

"I know that." I drew a breath. "But your daughter is forty-one years—"

"I still preside over this house."

"No, you don't," I countered. "This is Sadie's house."

"A woman doesn't preside." He waved his hand dismissively, and then, his eyes boring into mine, added, "You know, Jim, when I first met you years ago, I wasn't terribly impressed."

I folded my arms across my chest. "Yes, I sensed that."

"Now it appears that, while you claim to be a practicing Mormon, you began dating my daughter knowing that she writes anti-

Mormon pornography."

"I love your daughter and her book isn't anti-Mormon pornography."

"It most certainly is, and the fact that you don't recognize that speaks volumes about your character. Which is why I checked you out."

"You *checked me out?*"

"With your former bishops."

"Bishops aren't supposed to give out—"

"They can to other bishops."

"But only in an emergency or if there's been a crime—"

"So your father left when you were four and your sister was two."

"Actually, Kellie was eighteen months old."

"Your mother went back to work and never remarried. Why not?"

"She ... I don't know. I was a kid at the time."

"Then I learned that you'd married, had a child, and then divorced because your wife wasn't, shall we say, *amorous* enough for you?"

My face flushed and the knot tightened in my stomach. "Who told you *that?*"

The president scowled. "That's confidential, of course."

"No. It's my personal life that's confidential."

"I can certainly see why you'd like it to be. I found your clothes in my daughter's bedroom just now."

Seething, I stared back at his self-satisfied face. "You snooped around your grown daughter's bedroom?"

"The point is that, based on your enthusiasm over my daughter's pornographic books, your familiarity with her bedroom, and your overall history with women, I can easily conclude that you're only after one thing."

"This is outrageous!" I jumped to my feet.

The front door flew open and Sadie blew into the room. One

look at my face and she knew. "I told you not to talk to him, Jim." She glared down at the president. "Daddy, get the hell out of my house."

"I'm not through," he insisted.

"You know you're not welcome here without Mom."

"Your mother is away, and thanks to you, far too ill to return anytime soon. You're practically killing her—"

"According to you, I've been practically killing her for the past thirty years. Ever since I came home from that sleepover with my ears pierced."

"Sadie ... sir." I held up a hand toward each of them. "I think this would be a good time for us all to go to our corners and calm down."

They both ignored my suggestion.

President Gordon pointed at me. "This man is a sex addict."

"Give me a break," Sadie spat. "What'd you do, call up an old bishop of his, one who isn't getting any?"

"He's only after one thing."

Now blindly furious, I stepped in front of Sadie, stared down at her father, and pointed at the door. "She just told you to leave. Now get *out*," I shouted.

"Please, Jim." Sadie tugged my arm. "Let me handle this."

I reluctantly let her pull me aside.

"Jim, will you please walk around the block and give me a minute to talk to him alone?" she asked.

Leave her alone with this bully? "No, Sadie, I won't do that."

She stared at me, her eyes pleading. When I wouldn't back down, she turned to her father. "Okay, I've heard your opinion, Dad. Now you either leave or you'll get to hear mine."

The president remained rigidly in place on the sofa. "You're an ungrateful daughter who's made yet another in a series of bad choices."

"And you're a controlling, selfish man who raised his six children in a cult," Sadie replied.

My mouth fell open and President Gordon came to his feet.

"The Mormon Church is not a cult," the president boomed.

"It *is* a cult." Sadie took a step toward her father. "And it was founded by a lying, manipulative womanizer who wrote one of the most boring novels in history and then passed it off as scripture."

I sank into a chair.

"Joseph Smith was a prophet of God," said President Gordon.

"He was a misogynist who demanded sex from a fourteen-year-old girl and stole other men's wives," Sadie retorted. "*He* was the sex addict, not my boyfriend."

"I'm not listening to these *abominations*." President Gordon strode angrily to the door and yanked it open.

"Then get out!" she hollered after him. "And don't come back without Mom."

Sadie shut the door behind her father, walked partway back into the room, and then stopped. An ocean of silence washed over us.

"I'm sorry, Jim," she said finally. "I had to push his buttons. It's the only way he'd leave without being physically forced."

I stared back at her, flummoxed.

"If I'd let you hit him, my mother would never have forgiven me," she added.

"Did you really think I'd deck your old man? For crying out loud, he's in his seventies."

"My brother-in-law belted him."

I stood up slowly, trying to get my bearings. "He *broke in* the back door. He helped himself to our dinner."

"I know, Jim."

"He called my old bishops. At least one of them told him that I'm this ... sex fiend."

"According to my father, he said that."

"It bothers me that your father thinks I'm only after one thing."

Sadie let loose a disgusted sigh. "He also thinks ancient Jews built boats and sailed to America." Her face paled. "Sorry, Jim."

I smirked. "That's a line from the *Book of Mormon* musical."

She walked toward me, closing the gap between us. "It is. And

I love that you know that. You're a whole different kind of Mormon than my dad."

"Uh-huh. Meaning, at least, that in order to push my buttons you'll need to invent some fresh material."

"Maxwell, I don't want to push your buttons. That's why I asked you to walk around the block."

We stared at each other, neither of us moving.

Finally I threw up my hands. "For crying out loud. What just happened here?"

"My father just happened here."

Sadie swept up the glass in the kitchen and I went to the hardware store for materials to board up the window. Upon my return, I did a makeshift repair of the door while she silently prepared our dinner. Then, seated across from each other at the dining room table, we struggled with small talk over our vegetable soup. Having evidently abandoned her diet, Sadie went through two bowls of soup, half of the pasta salad I'd picked up, and a couple of thick pieces of French bread. I, on the other hand, barely finished my single serving. Despite our different appetites, we finished at the same time, leaving us to lean back and smile awkwardly.

"I'll do the dishes," Sadie offered. Her hands trembled as she took our bowls to the kitchen.

"Why not let me?" I stood and collected our silverware and glasses, set them on the counter next to the sink, and then said automatically, "That was a nice dinner."

"No, it wasn't." Sadie dropped the bowls in the kitchen sink. When they shattered she burst into tears. "It's ruined all over again. Just like back in college."

I pulled her into my arms. She buried her head in the crook of my neck and sobbed. "It was never going to work," she choked.

"Yes, it will." I stroked her hair. "We'll make it work."

"But our families, the church…"

"We're star crossed lovers, just like Romeo and Juliet."

She looked up at me. "They both died."

"I was just trying to lighten the mood."

"Oh, Jim." Sadie shook her head. "I'm sorry I said those things about the church. But I can't take them back, and I know you hate me for them."

"Sadie, I could never hate you." Then, less convincingly, I added, "You only did it to get rid of him. I understand."

"Believe it or not, I was trying to stick up for you."

"I do believe that, Sadie."

"When the time comes, will you stick up for me?" she asked.

Surprised and suddenly angry, I backed away from her. "What do you mean *will* I?" A voice in my head silenced me. It sounded a lot like Mom. I drew a breath and continued quietly, "Sadie, I've done nothing *but* stick up for you over the past few days."

She started to speak and then stopped, perhaps listening to a voice in her own head. I could see that we were at a crossroads, poised to venture into dangerous territory. Hoping to change direction, I slipped an arm around her waist and wiped the tears from her cheeks. She blinked and more ran down my fingers. "I'm exhausted by the drama, aren't you?" I asked.

"Yes." Sadie nodded and assumed a slight air of formality. "No more dramatics." Stepping to the sink, she gathered the broken dishes, tossed them in the trash, and then rinsed the silverware for me to put in the dishwasher.

I handed her our water glasses, noticing for the first time that she hadn't poured herself any wine. I wondered if she had suddenly become self-conscious about drinking in front of me.

"Want to watch some TV?" she asked me.

"Sure."

Sitting side-by-side on the couch, I flipped channels until we settled on the movie, *Game Change,* about the 2008 McCain/Palin campaign. I thought it was a bit too partisan toward the left but didn't comment, as I figured Sadie probably felt otherwise. But whatever she thought, she kept it to herself, affording us none of our usual back and forth over politics. Only handholding and mild reactions at the appropriate places.

My attention alternated between the TV and the memory of the exchange with President Gordon. How different Sadie's home life had been from mine. I wondered if her father was the real reason Sadie had left the church. It wouldn't surprise me, given his bad example. I wanted to tell her that most Mormons weren't like him. That he was the antithesis of what a good Latter-day Saint father should be. But the voice in my head, the one that sounded like Mom, told me to be still on the subject.

When the film ended we both declared ourselves too tired for the late evening news and retired upstairs to bed. I pulled her to me beneath the covers and whispered, "Things will be better in the morning."

"I hope so, Maxwell."

We kissed and then rolled onto our separate sides, just like an old married couple.

Only we weren't married. That reality suddenly and savagely flooded my brain. How had my standards sunk so low and so quickly? In spite of her coarse and intrusive manner, my sister had been right. Bishop Haas, too. Even Whitney. And if I were to ask him, Bishop Wu would get right in line with them. For crying out loud, since when did Jim Maxwell sleep with a woman he wasn't married to? Since when did Jim Maxwell donate sperm to lesbians? I buried my face in my pillow until I couldn't breathe, and then, gasping for air, rolled onto my back. What hurt most were Sadie's words to her father earlier. She was right. She couldn't take them back. And while I could never hate her, I was deeply upset over what she'd said.

It's not that I entirely disagreed. Of course Joseph Smith practiced polygamy. And informed sources confirmed that some of his wives were underage and that others were already married. I knew that. But I never let it bother me. Why go down that road? The man translated the Book of Mormon, for crying out loud.

"The word of God," I said aloud. Then, turning to see that

Sadie was still sleeping, I added silently to myself, *not the most boring novel in history.*

I dug my knuckles into my eyes. All along I'd been telling myself that proposing now would be too much like those whirlwind BYU courtships we both disdained. But the truth was, deep in the back of my mind, I knew our marriage would never work. Sure, she had a nice figure and a pretty face and she managed to make me laugh. Also the sex was fantastic.

I let out a sigh of disgust. Was that all we had? In the absence of common beliefs and mutual respect, did it all come down to sex? Had President Gordon seen what I couldn't? Was I really only after one thing? The voice in my head, the one that sounded like Mom, immediately and loudly objected. I inhaled a couple of deep breaths, pulling myself together. I knew what Sadie and I had was far more than just physical.

That being said, how could I be with a woman who had such a low opinion of my beliefs? How could I respect somebody who wasn't worthy to go to the temple? I would be rejecting everything I'd learned in seminary, in Sunday School, on my mission.

On the other hand, how could I align myself with Kellie, President Gordon, Whitney, and Bishop Haas, all of whom shared my beliefs but had no regard for my feelings for Sadie, not to mention my privacy? I stared at the ceiling in the darkened room. What if there was no longer a place for me, either in or out of the church?

I reached over and rested my hand on Sadie's back. She was breathing steadily, clearly asleep, or clearly wanting me to think she was. It occurred to me that, up until now, I had assumed that, deep down, Sadie still believed, and that she might even come back to the Church one day. Now any hope of that was dead. Nevertheless, I still respected her. In spite of her ugly words about the church and in spite of the fact that she would never go to the temple. I literally ached with love for her. But was love enough?

My mind fretted for what seemed like hours until exhaustion gradually took hold. At last I drifted off, only to see Mom, the fog eclipsing all but her face. "Follow your heart, Jimmy," she said and then disappeared entirely.

17

Sunday morning I awoke alone, still weary after a fitful night. My mobile phone told me the time was nine thirty-seven and the smell of coffee hinted that Sadie was in the kitchen. I went to the bathroom to shave, shower, and slip into jeans and a clean overpriced tee shirt. Then I headed downstairs.

Sadie was in her bathrobe at the kitchen table, her hands wrapped around a coffee mug. Behind her, the board covering the broken pane blocked out the sun, casting the room in an unnatural gloom.

She smiled up at me, her expression soft and void of dimples. "I didn't feel like making breakfast this morning."

"You know I don't expect you to."

"There's juice in the fridge, the other half of the grapefruit, also cereal, and a couple kinds of bread for toast."

I sat down next to her. "I'm not hungry."

Her face fell. "You wouldn't eat last night either. You're still angry with me, aren't you?"

"No. I'm just ... you called the Mormon Church a cult."

"Because I knew it would push my dad's buttons."

"The stuff about the prophet Joseph?"

"My language was overly harsh, I admit." Sadie reached for my hand, her skin felt warm from the coffee mug. "But surely you knew that Joseph Smith had a number of plural wives, some of whom were teenagers?"

"I'd read that, yeah," I admitted.

"The church published an essay on the subject."

"I know. I read that, too. But do you also think the Book of Mormon is just a boring novel?"

"No." She shook her head. "I only put it that way to tick off my father. I know it's much more than that to a lot of people. Just not to me."

"So you think it's a work of fiction?"

"Jim, I know I told you I left because I was offended and wanted to sin."

"You mean because you're a free spirit."

"It's true, I am," she repeated slowly. "Even so, if I still believed that the Book of Mormon was the word of God, I'd be in church every Sunday, like you are. I don't believe anymore, and I can't change that, not even for you." She squeezed my hand. "I won't be a hypocrite, Jim."

Pausing to take in her beautiful face, I realized I couldn't stop loving her if I tried. "I don't want you to change, Sadie."

She smiled weakly. "Speaking of church, Bishop Wu invited you. Meetings start at eleven, remember?"

"You think I should go this morning?"

"Why not? Your church clothes are still in my closet where you left them last Sunday. Change, have a bite to eat, and you can still make it in plenty of time for the opening prayer."

"And what will you do while I'm in church for three hours?"

"Read the paper, have a hot shower, lounge around in my sweats and otherwise amuse myself in the manner of all sinners."

I stroked her cheek. "You're not a sinner."

"You sure about that?"

"With all my heart."

A hint of a dimple surfaced in her cheek. "When you get back we can cook supper. Just like Sunday after church ought to be."

Squeezing her hand, I looked into her gorgeous eyes and said, "That sounds like something I could get used to."

"Me, too."

We were gravitating toward a kiss when my mobile jolted us apart. I pulled it from my pants pocket. Julia.

"Kiddo."

"Can I come see you, Dad?"

My watch read ten fifteen. "Aren't you in church?"

"I snuck out. Bishop Franklin wants to interview me today. I really, really don't want to talk to him."

I stood up from the table and paced into the living room. "Why not, honey?"

"I just don't. C'mon, Dad, you don't want to talk to your bishop either, right?"

Shutting my eyes, I pinched the bridge of my nose.

"Will you meet me at the Caltrain station in San Francisco?" she whined.

"Caltrain?" My eyes blinked open. "Where are you?"

"At the bus stop by the Safeway on Almaden Expressway."

"Forget the bus. Wait for me inside Safeway." I hung up and jogged back to the kitchen. "Sadie, I've got to go. It's Julia." I turned and hurried to the door.

"What's wrong?"

"She's having a crisis," I called over my shoulder.

Sadie followed me onto the porch. "Drive safely."

I sped down the peninsula, scolding myself for neglecting my daughter. For days now she'd been trying to get out of her meeting with Bishop Franklin, but I'd been too self-absorbed to deal with it.

Of course Julia didn't want to meet with her bishop. No Mormon kid wanted to. Especially when he or she had something embarrassing to confess. But all Mormon kids had to fess up, just like their parents had to fess up. That was, unless the Mormon kid's dad was avoiding his own bishop because he was sleeping with his ex-Mormon girlfriend. In that case, the Mormon kid might have a good excuse for slipping out of the ordeal herself.

"Damn it," I cursed aloud and then pounded the steering wheel. I loved Sadie, but ever since she'd walked back into my life, I'd been encased in this romantic fog, completely blind to reason, and the result had been nothing but chaos. Three weeks ago I had been a single and obediently celibate Mormon man, a good brother, a doting uncle and, above all, a devoted father. Fast forward a few days and suddenly I was having an affair, donating my sperm to lesbians, and—in the mind of my ex-wife—still married. On top of that, I was on the verge of estrangement from my sister and nephews, and possibly facing church discipline. That was, if my bishop ever caught up with me. Meanwhile, my daughter, acting on my example, was avoiding her own bishop. I cursed and pounded the steering wheel again. Sure I loved Sadie. Marcia, too. But was love enough? Was love worth any of this?

I exited the freeway and breezed through light traffic on the expressway. When I pulled into the Safeway lot my daughter ran straight for my car. I shifted to park and hit the unlock button.

"Julia," I said once she'd climbed into the front seat, "why don't you want to talk to Bishop Franklin?"

"I just don't." She looked out the passenger side window. "Can't you just trust me, Dad?"

I unhooked my seatbelt and rested my hand on her shoulder. "I do trust you, kiddo. But I'm worried. Is there a problem? Something you need to tell me about?"

She was still turned away from me, but through the reflection on the window I could see her tightly shut her eyes. "He's going to ask about ... masturbation."

I felt a rush of relief. When I entertained the list of nightmare scenarios, masturbation didn't even make the top tier, although its mention did inspire an indecorous reminder of my recent appointment at the sperm bank.

Julia's voice trembled. "There's this boy in fourth period. He's a nonmember."

I nodded, wanting to ask the kid's name but holding my tongue.

"I mean, it's not like we're going together. He barely knows I'm alive."

My hand reached over to stroke her hair and then rested on her shaking shoulder. "Stupid boy then."

A smile flashed across her face as she shook her head. "No, he's really cool, Dad, and he's nice, too. Nicer than the boys at church."

"If you like him, he must be nice."

"Only sometimes when I think about him I feel like…" She drew a jagged breath.

"Touching yourself?" I said gently.

"Right. But I don't. Not when I'm awake. Only sometimes I'll have dreams and then wake up and I'm—"

"That's natural, honey."

"At Standards Night, Bishop Franklin said it wasn't."

"Really?" This guy really was over-the-top. "Remember, you don't have to agree with him."

Julia frowned. A tear slid down her cheek.

I leaned over and kissed her hair. "When he asks, just tell him you're morally clean. You don't need to go into detail, and you certainly don't need to tell him about your dreams." I chuckled. "In fact, I'm fairly certain he won't want to know about them."

She stared back at me, her reddened eyes widening. "Oh, yes, he does. He said so when he pulled me aside at Standards Night."

My breath caught in my throat. "He pulled you aside?"

"He wanted to know why I hadn't signed up to meet with him."

Julia wiped a tear from her cheek. "I said I didn't need to meet with him." Her voice faltered and she choked back a sob.

I handed her my handkerchief. She used it to blow her nose.

"Julia, did Bishop Franklin actually say he wanted to hear about your dreams?"

She nodded. "He did, Dad, honest. My dreams, my impure thoughts. Then he warned me."

"Warned you, how?"

"To not avoid his questions, because he receives inspiration and I don't." She blew into handkerchief again. "Please don't make me meet with him, Dad."

"*Make* you meet with him? Not on your life."

She threw her arms around my neck. I held her to me, clamping down my anger. Best to save it for the proper time and place.

"You did the right thing, coming to me with this, kiddo." I leaned back and used my thumb to brush a tear from her cheek.

"It seems wrong not to obey the bishop," Julia said, her voice returning to its normal cadence. "But then, going along with him feels even more wrong."

"That's because Bishop Franklin is wrong." I rested my hand on her shoulder and looked into her eyes. In this light they were as blue as cornflowers. "He's wrong to suggest you have something to confess. He's wrong to ask you or any of the young women such inappropriate questions. And he's wrong when he says you can't receive inspiration on your own behalf. You did, in fact, just this morning."

Julia smiled slightly. "I guess so, yeah."

"Honey, it's important to listen to our church leaders and to take their counsel, but not to the extent that we give up control of our own lives. Don't forget that, okay?"

"Okay, Dad."

I smoothed her hair with my hand, remembering back to when I used to untangle it with a comb. My anger resurfaced. "That creep Franklin has some nerve."

"Will you tell him that, Dad?"

"Oh, yeah." I fastened my seatbelt and asked her to do the same. Then, shifting into gear, I drove us the few blocks to her ward meetinghouse.

On our way there, Julia asked, "Do you really love Sadie?"

"Yes."

"Then you should get married."

Out the corner of my eye, I saw her smiling like it was Christmas morning.

"Just ask her, Dad."

"Not sure it's the right thing to do, kiddo."

"Why not, Dad? Is it something Bishop Haas said? Or Mom? Or Aunt Kellie?"

I kept my eyes on the road.

We arrived a few minutes before the end of the meetings. "Go find your mother in Relief Society and tell her what you told me."

"You mean about Jake in fourth period?"

Jake. So that was the little twit's name. "Tell her what Bishop Franklin said when he pulled you aside at Standards Night."

Julia made a face.

"Don't worry, honey. Mom will be on our side on this."

I walked into the foyer, conspicuous in my jeans and tee shirt. Right off, I spotted the creep. He was a couple of inches taller than me, but I was ten years younger and a good thirty pounds heavier. If I had to, I could take him.

"Why, Jim—"

"Stay away from my daughter, Franklin."

"What's wrong?"

"She's not answering any of your perverted questions."

His face paled. "I'm sure I don't know what you mean."

"I mean how you feel *inspired* to grill her about the dreams she has at night," I shouted, happy to see we had drawn attention.

"Her *thoughts*, Jim. Only her impure thoughts."

"Uh-huh, and alone in a room with you."

"Well … that's how it's done."

"It sure is." I jabbed my finger at his face. "Go near Julia and I'll beat the crap out of you."

I strode out of the building, onlookers scurrying to clear my path to the door.

Julia and her mom were waiting for me by my car. Before I could say anything, Whitney thanked me. She was as pretty as she was the day we met, and dressed in blue, her best color. But again, all I could feel for her was sadness.

"Take Julia home," I told her. "I'll call later."

I wrapped my arms around my daughter, overwhelmed with love for her. "Proud of you," I said.

As I watched them disappear around the side of the building, I wondered if it might be best if Julia came to church with me from now on. No telling how Whitney might react to that suggestion. One thing at a time, I told myself, and was reaching in my pocket for my keys when an intense image flooded my brain. Mom and I were sitting on my bed in the old house on Lambert. I was in my penguin pajamas with the feet. Mom was reading me her favorite scripture from the New Testament.

I unlocked the car with my remote, dug my scriptures out of the pile in my backseat, and climbed into the front. Quickly turning to First Corinthians, chapter thirteen, I read aloud:

"Though I speak with the tongues of men and of angels, and have not charity, I am become as sounding brass or a tinkling cymbal."

I fell silent and stared at the page while Mom's clear, strong voice recited the rest of the chapter through to the final verse:

"And now abideth faith, hope, charity, these three; but the greatest is charity."

I looked up to see commotion swirling around me. Church had let out and families were piling into their cars. They might have been light years away. I closed my eyes and listened to Mom repeat the verses in my brain, only this time using her own words.

"Charity is pure love, Jimmy, and love never fails. Love bears all things and endures all things. In the end, love is what matters. That's why you must always follow your heart. *Please* follow your heart, Jimmy."

"I will, Mom," I whispered, and paused to let the warmth wash over me. In that moment—thanks to my mom and those thirteen verses Paul had penned to the Corinthians—I knew precisely what I had to do. And here was the kicker. Not one of those thirteen verses had made it onto the official Scripture Mastery list.

Minutes later, I was back on 280 to San Francisco, my mind set and my conscience clear. I no longer cared about winning anyone's approval, not Bishops Haas' or Wu's, not President Gordon's, and certainly not Whitney's. I loved my sister, Kellie. But I could only go so far to please her. I was, after all, her *older* brother. It was time we both remembered that.

The problem was I'd been complacent, too settled in my situation, too apt to let others take charge. Blind to the dangers around me, I'd become those characters in the Sunday School analogies. The frog languishing in his own stew, the driver skirting the cliff's edge. Content with shuffling the preprogrammed verses, I'd been missing the whole text. And, thanks to my complacency, I had almost made the biggest mistake of my life. Again.

Was love enough? Of course love wasn't *enough*—love was everything. It was out of love that I donated my sperm to my best friend and her wife. It was out of love that I cancelled my daughter's meeting with her bishop. It was out of love that I remained a faithful Mormon. It was out of love that I was no longer celibate. And it was out of love that I wanted to be married again.

Was love worth it? Hell, yes! Love was worth the disapproval of a dozen bishops, the full extent of my sister's wrath, and even a daily rerun of Sadie's tirade at her dad. It was worth all of Whitney's manipulations and every long, furtive look from the women in the fertility center waiting room. It was worth a closetful of overpriced tee shirts, a weeklong Woody Allen marathon, and enough Mormon wedding receptions to empty the bathroom scales off the shelves at Target. It was worth a visit to the Seagull Bar and the whole gamut of Julia's knowing looks. It was worth my heart.

Honestly, what the heck had I been waiting for? Like Mom predicted, I'd known in a heartbeat that Sadie was the one. I should have proposed right then, at the wedding reception, or afterward, at the Starbucks. At the ex-Mormon party, on Ocean Beach, at the Wharf in front of those out-of-towners who mistook me for an aspiring porn star. All this time had slipped by when I should have been doing right by her.

I raced past the airport and up to the City, pushing the speed limit, mentally making up for lost time. But as I neared her house, a tremor of fear shuddered through to my heart. *If she'll have me*, I reminded myself. After all, this grand scheme for my eternal happiness could only go forward if she said yes.

Sadie came to the door in pajama bottoms and a sweatshirt, her hair still damp from the shower. She looked gorgeous.

"Things okay?" she asked, closing the door behind me.

"That's up to you." I cupped her face in my hands. "Will you marry me, Sadie?"

Her beautiful eyes widened and she placed her hands on my shoulders. "Are you sure, Maxwell?"

I nodded, my breath caught in my throat.

"You do get that I'm never going back to the church."

"That's not important to me anymore," I said, choking back emotion. "All that matters is I love you, Sadie, exactly as you are, and with my whole heart. Please say you'll have me."

"Well, in that case." Those adorable dimples appeared on her cheeks. "I thought you'd never ask."

Wrapping my arms around her, I sang out, "She said yes!" Then I lifted her in the air and swung her around in circle after circle as our laughter echoed through the house. Everything was going to work out in heaven, I reminded myself. That's why it's heaven. Then I realized—I was already there.

The Unabridged Journal of Julia Camilla Maxwell
Sunday, October 27
9:15 p.m.

Best Sabbath ever. I don't know what dad said to Bishop Franklin but bottom line, I don't have to meet with him. As far as Mom's concerned, I don't ever have to see him again. Who would have thought that my bonkers parents would reunite for one afternoon and come through for me like this?

Dad was so cool today. Even after I told him about Jake. Mom too, although she still doesn't know about Jake—no sense pushing it.

But she made me a really yummy dinner tonight. For the first time in days Mom said nice things about Dad and nothing about Sadie or porn or our eternal fate. She didn't even object when I suggested I might want to attend Dad's Willow Glen ward. (Of course, I left out how Bishop Haas might be excommunicating him.)

"Anything to avoid that creep Franklin," she'd said. It was amazing. Things were almost like … normal. Although, after we'd finished the dinner dishes, Mom did go for an absurdly long run on her treadmill.

Then I came in my room just now and saw my cellphone blinking. I had a voicemail from Dad: "Sadie and I are engaged. Will call with details tomorrow. Love you, kiddo."

Oh my gosh!!! Dad's getting married to Sadie! How great is that? Now he doesn't have to talk to the bishop or get excommunicated. He can stop avoiding Aunt Kellie. And I'm about to be the luckiest stepdaughter ever!

Maybe I can even go to church in San Francisco. See what this Bishop Woo is like. From the way Mom was going on, he seemed almost reasonable. Maybe he can explain the whole polygamy in heaven business to me. I'm probably getting ahead of myself here. But seriously this is the best news! Better than if Jake were to ask me to the prom. Well, maybe not. Okay, now I'm really getting ahead of myself.

Life is just about perfect right now. I intend to soak in the moment, put on my headphones and dance around to Coldplay and Rihanna. Then later when I say my prayers I will first thank Heavenly Father for making my dad so happy. I'll thank Him for giving me such a wonderful new stepmom. Then after that I'll beg Him that I might be as far away as possible when my mother finally and predictably blows her top.

18

Monday I dialed Kellie.

"Hi, Jim, we missed seeing you at church yesterday. For Sunday dinner, too."

"Sorry, sis. I've been up at Sadie's house."

"James Widtsoe Maxwell, nothing I've said means anything to you, does it?"

"Not lately, no."

"What about what our mother might have to say?"

"Our mother would say, 'I'm glad he's finally found her.' I think you know that already."

"I know nothing of the—"

"Oh, I think you do. She'd also tell us to stay close and take care of each other. I'm sure you know that. And I intend to stay close, Kellie. I'm still your brother, whether or not you approve of my choices." Before she could respond I added, "From here on, if you can't be happy for Sadie and me you can keep your opinions to yourself."

After a pause, Kellie replied, "Are you through?"

"No. There's more."

"What now?"

"We're getting married at City Hall on Wednesday."

She heaved a sigh. "Anything else?"

"Yes. I've donated sperm so Marcia and her wife can have a baby."

The line fell silent.

"That's it," I said.

"Are you sure?"

"For now, yes."

"Goodbye, Jimmy."

"Bye, Kel."

19

On Wednesday afternoon we were climbing the steps of the San Francisco City Hall. Sadie looked gorgeous in her silky beige dress, Marcia and Cathy looked smart in purple, Julia was pretty in pink, and I sported a suit that wasn't from Target.

Three weeks ago I'd been sticking with the same old drill, content with my single, celibate existence, and wholly unaware that I was about to marry the woman of my dreams. Who would have believed it? Sadie and I finally had our whirlwind BYU courtship. Twenty-two years later.

Bob and Harvey, the couple ahead of us, said they'd been together for fifteen years. As we were congratulating them a text came in from Kellie: *I'm glad you've found her. The two of you for dinner a week from Sunday?*

I showed Sadie. She smiled and nodded, and I texted back: *We're there.*

And then before I knew it, I was kissing my beautiful bride. Marcia, Cathy, and Julia were applauding, and in my mind's eye, I could see Mom twirling on Ocean Beach, the light from heaven shining down upon her.

About the Author

Donna Banta is author of the novels, *The Girls from Fourth Ward* and *False Prophet*. She earned a degree in English from Brigham Young University and was married in the Mormon temple in Oakland, California. For years she tried to remain active in the LDS Church as a "Mormon Feminist," an effort that led to her premature release from practically every ward position she was called to fill. Now she's just a feminist and her calling is writing. She lives in San Francisco with her husband.